Gertrude, Gumshoe: Slam Is Murder

R.E. MERRILL

New Creation Publishing

1

Gertrude rushed out of her trailer, leaving the door flapping behind her. Cats spilled out in her wake, scattering in a blur of fur. Gertrude flew down her steps and hurried toward Calvin's trailer, two doors down.

She was moving quite swiftly, given her abilities, but of course, she had her walker, so she looked a little like a large orange-haired rabbit hopping across the trailer park.

She arrived out of breath and rapped on Calvin's door.

"What?" Calvin called out from within.

"It's me, Gertrude!"

"I know. What do you want?"

"Calvin! Let me in! I got the date!"

There was a bit of banging from within and then the door opened. "What date?"

Gertrude used her walker to push past him into his trailer. "The date for my driver's test. What else?"

Calvin shut the door and turned to face her.

"What does that have to do with me?"

"I just thought you'd be happy. If I get a driver's license, you won't have to drive me around ... as much."

Calvin walked by her and returned to his recliner. "As you've made it painfully clear in the past, even if you get a driver's license, you still won't have a car."

"What do you mean *if?*"

Calvin rolled his eyes as he reclined. "I believe my meaning was clear. I'm not really convinced you will be successful at this endeavor. Why are you holding a newspaper?"

"What?" Gertrude looked down at her hands. One hand clutched her letter from the Bureau of Motor Vehicles. The other held the newspaper. "Oh, this," she said, remembering. "Yes, this is the real reason I'm here, but now you've ruffled my feathers will all your nasty doubts."

He didn't seem to feel terrifically guilty about the alleged feather-ruffling. "Is that newspaper recent, or is it from your collection?"

Gertrude was incensed. "You know what? I don't know why I put up with you. I came over here with two handfuls of exciting news, and you have ruined my parade!" She turned and stalked haughtily to the door.

"It's rained on my parade, Gertrude."

Gertrude stopped and looked over her shoulder. "What?"

"It's rained, not ruined. Now, tell me what's in the newspaper."

Gertrude considered her options. She wanted to stay mad. She also wanted to tell him about their new case. She decided she could be angry later. She returned to the living room and plopped down on Calvin's couch.

"Have a seat," Calvin muttered.

"Thanks. I just did. So, I brought you this paper because I think we need to go to Portland."

Calvin guffawed. "Oh! Portland! Of course!"

"Calvin, there isn't any crime here. No one has been kidnapped or murdered for months!"

"Well isn't that a shame. And someone has been kidnapped or murdered in Portland?"

Gertrude unfolded the newspaper. "I think so."

"You *think* so?"

"Well, I heard about one suspicious death on the news. Then, in the paper, I saw another suspicious death that occurred the very next night. Now, the news didn't connect the two—"

"But you did?"

"Yessirree. I got on Facebook and found out that these two were at the very same event the night before the first one died. The other one died the very next night. Coincidence? I think not."

"What was the event?" Calvin looked intrigued.

"A poetry slam."

"A what?"

3

"It's a competition poetry reading. People read poems and judges judge them. Someone wins."

"How do you know this?"

"I read the description on the Facebook event page."

"You're turning into quite the Facebook aficionado, aren't you?"

Gertrude nodded. "I'm not sure how anyone ever solved crimes without Facebook."

Calvin smirked. "Indeed. So I suppose you want me to take you to Portland?"

"Yep. I've got a plan. My driver's test isn't until Wednesday, but the next poetry slam is on Monday. So I'll need you to take me. I'm going undercover."

Calvin guffawed again. "Undercover? As what? A poet?"

"Yes. As a poet."

Calvin barked out another round of laughter. His face grew red, and tears began to leak out of the corners of his closed eyes.

Gertrude wanted to slap him. "I'm not sure why that's so funny."

Calvin took a deep, albeit shaky, breath and said, "I'm just not sure it's necessary for you to be a poet. I mean, can't we just go to the poetry reading as spectators? Do you really need to *participate?*" He pushed out this last word, which sent him into another fit of giggles.

"Calvin, stop tee-heeing like a little girl. I've given this some thought, and I think it would be a little weird if we just show up as spectators and start asking questions, but if we *participate*"—she mocked his use of the word—"then we have more of a reason to be nosey. Just trust me on this. I know what I'm doing."

Calvin took another deep breath and this time seemed to have gained control of his emotions. He wiped at his eyes with the back of one hand. "All right then. Let me see the paper."

She hoisted herself off the couch and crossed the small room to hand him the opened newspaper. He took it, and then she leaned in and pointed to the article she wanted him to see.

"Ah, got a big headline, I see."

"No, not yet," Gertrude said, completely missing his irony. "They don't know yet that it was a murder."

"And you do?"

"Just read."

Calvin read. But not for long. "Gertrude, this says he died of alcohol poisoning. That's not suspicious."

"But," Gertrude said, pointing at the paper, "his blood alcohol level was only 0.25 percent. That's not enough to kill a person, Calvin."

"How do you know?"

"I looked it up on the Internet. With my jitterbug."

Calvin looked up at her, though her face was hovering only inches from his own. "Why? You saw this article about a kid drinking himself to death, and you just thought you should investigate blood alcohol levels?"

"I was looking for a case. And I already knew about the girl who died the night before. She was from the same college."

"You were looking for a case," Calvin repeated incredulously, seeming not to hear the rest of Gertrude's explanation. "Gertrude, I know I've said this before, but maybe you should find a new hobby."

"Calvin, there are two dead 'kids,' as you call them, in Portland. You really want to ignore that?"

Calvin sighed. "OK, show me the other one."

"I can't. She's not in the paper. I saw her on the news. But you can find her on the Internet if you want."

"No, thanks. I don't want to get out of my chair. Why don't you just tell me about her?" He handed her the paper.

She took it and returned to her spot on the couch. "The first victim's name is Abby Livingstone. She died the night before John did. In a car accident—"

"Gertrude, a car accident is not suspicious!"

"Would you let me finish? She was drinking too, and she supposedly drove her car off a bridge. But I'm telling you, Calvin, they are at the same college—"

"They are *at* the same college? As in right now?"

"Well not right now because they're both dead."

Calvin sighed. "No, I mean, they were going to college now? It's July!"

"That's what the news said. Now, will you let me finish? So, same college, they were both at the same event on Monday night, and then they both die of alcohol related causes within 24 hours of each other? Something isn't right."

"I agree. Something isn't right with the amount of alcohol college kids consume nowadays. Of course, they can afford to because my tax dollars are paying for their tuition. If they had to pay for it themselves, they probably would be more—"

"Calvin," Gertrude interrupted, "let's not get distracted. The point is, we've got two dead youngsters on our hands. I think they knew each other. Let's just go to this poetry thing and check it out. Maybe it will amount to nothing. Maybe we'll get to catch another murderer."

"Gertrude, Portland is a hundred miles away. And there will be tolls. I'm not sure I want to commit to this. Can't you find a crime closer to home?"

"I'll pay for the tolls."

Calvin snorted. "Sure you will. Tell you what. I'll think about it. We have until Monday to decide, correct?"

"Yes, that's correct. But you need to make up your mind because I don't want to bother writing poems if you're just going to chicken out."

Calvin rolled his eyes. "If you've got time to sparc, shouldn't you be studying for your driver's test?"

2

On Sunday morning, Gertrude decided she should go to church. She hadn't been in a long time, and she had grown tired of both studying the driver's manual and trying to write poems.

She called the CAP bus, hoping that Norm was driving. The CAP bus, a van provided by the nonprofit Community Action Program, was driven by volunteers, and Norm was her favorite.

The van pulled up in front of her trailer. It wasn't Norm. It was Andrea. Gertrude groaned. She didn't like Andrea one bit. Andrea was a detail-oriented, retired librarian who drove Gertrude crazy with her incessant dotting of i's and crossing of t's.

Hence, Gertrude only said, "Open Door Church" when she climbed into the van.

"Well, good morning to you too," Andrea snipped.

Gertrude didn't respond.

"I was actually hoping to see you," Andrea said.

"What?" Gertrude had never heard anything so surprising in her whole life.

"Yeah, you see, my cat died this week—"

Gertrude gasped. "Oh my, I am so sorry, Andrea!"

"Thank you. And I was wondering if you knew of any kittens. I just really need something to take my mind off ..." Her voice started to crack, and she trailed off.

"I have kittens—"

"You do?" Andrea cried, interrupting.

"Yep, cute little buggers too. But their mama is a Maine coon cat, so they might well grow up to be monsters." Gertrude snickered. "I call the mama Nor'easter. She was already pregnant when I got her. She came to me as a foster, though I almost always end up just keeping my foster cats. Most people don't want to adopt grown cats. Anyway, the kittens are ready to go, and you're welcome to one of them, as long as you promise to give him or her a loving home. And of course, get 'em fixed when they're old enough."

Andrea pulled into the parking lot of Open Door Church. She put the van in park and then turned to look at Gertrude. Her face was shiny with tears. "Thank you, Gertrude. I mean it. Thank you."

Gertrude became acutely uncomfortable. "Sure enough. If you're still on duty when church lets out, we can go pick out a kitten then."

Andrea nodded, smiling, even though tears were still sliding down her cheeks. "You bet. I'll be here."

Dumbfounded, Gertrude slid out of the van and headed toward the church without looking back. *Well I'll be. Andrea is part human after all.*

There weren't very many people at the church. Gertrude avoided eye contact all the way to her pew, as she didn't feel much like talking to anyone. Nevertheless, as she slid into her seat, she was accosted by Tiny.

"Gertrude!" he cried, startling her. Tiny was a giant of a man, but he often acted much like a child. Still facing her, he plopped down in the pew in front of her and she swore she felt the floor shake.

"Yes?"

"I need to hire you."

"What for?"

"Someone has stolen my food stamp card."

Gertrude's church also served as a homeless shelter, and Tiny lived there. Had been living there for quite a while, in fact.

"How's that work?" Gertrude asked. "Isn't your picture on the card?"

"Yes, but they never check it at the store. I just slide the card in the box and that's all I do."

"All right, Tiny, I'll look into it," Gertrude said.

"Really?"

"Really. Now scat."

"Wait. How much money will I have to pay you? I don't have much money."

"Don't worry about it, Tiny."

"Really?" Tiny stood up and Gertrude feared he was going to hug her. She wasn't sure she would survive such an encounter.

"I said that already, Tiny. Now scat, I need to talk to God."

Tiny nodded and lumbered off, and Gertrude let out a sigh of relief. She picked up a pew Bible and opened to Psalms. She didn't want to read, but she wanted to look busy lest anyone else try to talk to her.

The sermon was about dealing with anxiety. That wasn't something Gertrude could readily relate to, but she enjoyed the message just the same. She really liked her pastor.

When the service was over, she headed to the undercroft for some lunch. She usually didn't eat lunch at the church, but she wanted to look into Tiny's little problem.

They were serving spaghetti. Gertrude curled a lip up and looked around for someone helpful. Her eyes landed on Pete, who was standing in the spaghetti line.

"Hiya, Pete!" She sidled up to him, which spawned multiple accusations of cutting from those behind Pete in line. She turned to face them. "Oh, stop it! That'll be enough out of you. I'm not budging. I'm just talking to Peter here."

She looked up at Pete.

He looked down at her, managing to look both amused and anxious.

"Why do you look so nervous, Pete?"

"What do you want, Gertrude?"

She leaned toward him conspiratorially.

He leaned away from her.

She leaned toward him again.

"What?" he snapped.

"Someone's kifed Tiny's food stamp card," she whispered.

He waited for her to continue. When she didn't, he said, "And you think I did it?"

"No, of course not! But I thought you might have some idea who did."

Pete looked around. Everyone within ten feet was staring at them. "Let me sniff around. See what I can come up with."

"Well you need to hurry up."

"Why's that?" Pete asked.

"Because Tiny needs to eat."

Tiny passed them then, the spaghetti on his plate piled nearly a foot high.

"I think he'll be OK," Pete said.

3

"Oh my soul!" Andrea had just stepped inside Gertrude's trailer and was now standing stock still staring at Gertrude's collections in wonderment.

"Don't just stand there. Come on in. The kittens are back here."

Andrea followed Gertrude as she weaved through the stacks of her belongings toward the back of the trailer. They entered a narrow hallway made even tighter by the piles lining each wall. "I'd heard you were a hoarder, but this ..."

Gertrude stopped walking. She wanted to turn around and sizzle Andrea's face with her eyes, but there wasn't room to pivot. So she just looked over her shoulder. "I'm *not* a hoarder. I'm a *collector*. Now do you want this cat, or not?"

"Yes, yes, I do."

"All right then. Maybe you should be nice to me." Gertrude continued down the hallway until she got to the second doorway. Then she turned. "Welcome to the cats' room."

Andrea looked around. At the multiple litter boxes, which had been recently cleaned, the dozen scratching posts, the seemingly hundreds of cat toys, and the three vacuum cleaners lined neatly up against one wall. "Why do you have three vacuum cleaners?"

"You are an odd one, Andrea. Most people ask why I have twenty cats. Anyway, that one there," she said, pointing, "is the go-to machine. Works wonders on cat hair. The other two are parts machines.

Andrea laughed.

"Come on, Nor'easter and her babies are right over here." Gertrude headed toward a large cardboard box with a hole cut out of the front. It took her several seconds, but she managed to get down on her hands and knees and peer in. "Yep, she's in here," Gertrude said to Andrea, her head in the box, her rear sticking up in the air. "Hi there, Nor'easter," she cooed, "you sure are a pretty mama. Can I grab one of your babies here?" She reached in and scooped up a kitten, and then pulled him backward out of the box.

Andrea gasped.

Gertrude held the kitten up to her.

She took him in her arms, and he squeaked in protest. "They're still nursing?"

"A-yuh," Gertrude said, grunting as she used her walker to pull herself to her feet. Then she tried to catch her breath as she explained, "They're about eleven weeks old now, but they're eating solids too. They're ready to go, you can even get down there and look to see if there's another one more to your fancy, but you can also wait another week or so if you want. Then they should be done nursing altogether."

Andrea looked scared. "Do you think it's all right if I take her today?"

"You mean that one?" Gertrude asked, nodding toward the ball of fur Andrea currently had clutched to her chest.

Andrea nodded.

"He's a male."

"Oh!" Andrea looked down at him. "Guess I can't name you Cinderella!" She tittered.

Gertrude did not. "Yes, you can take him today. Just give him lots of cuddles. He's used to that. And that's the food he's been eating," she said, pointing toward the bags lined up against one wall.

"OK, I'll take him," Andrea said. "Do you mind if I put him back in for a second, though?"

Gertrude found that strange but stepped away from the box to let her do her thing. Andrea got down on all fours and placed the kitten back into the box. Then she stuck her head and one arm into the box. "Hi, there, Nor'easter," Andrea whispered. "My name is Andrea, and I'm going to take this little guy home with me. Is that OK? I just wanted you to meet me so that you could know that he's going to be all right. He's going to be great, in fact. Would that be all right with you? If I took your baby home to be my baby?" She paused.

A tear slid down Gertrude's cheek. She swatted it away.

"OK, then, thank you, Nor'easter. I sure do appreciate it. I'm going to name him Prince Charming."

Gertrude rolled her eyes.

"You're a beautiful mother, Nor'easter. Nice work." Andrea pulled her face out of the box. Her arm came out next, bringing Prince Charming with it.

Gertrude cleared her throat.

Andrea stood up, still looking down at her new friend.

"Well, you need to get going. I've got to study. Got a big test tomorrow."

"OK," Andrea said, not moving.

Gertrude headed toward the door, hoping Andrea would follow her.

She didn't.

Gertrude turned toward her. "Do you want some food to take with you?"

Andrea looked up at Gertrude standing near the door. This seemed to jolt her into action. "Nah, I can get some. Thank you, Gertrude." And finally, she made her way to the door.

With Andrea finally gone, Gertrude knew she should start studying for her driver's test, but she was too excited about the poetry slam. It was scarcely more than twenty-four hours away, and she still hadn't written a poem. She'd started several, but it was hard to get beyond that first line.

She decided that had to be her priority. She made her way into the kitchen and retrieved some paper and a pen out of her office supplies drawer. Then she sat down at the kitchen table. She spread the paper out in front of her and stared at it. Hail promptly jumped onto the table. She patted him. "Are you jealous? Are you jealous that Mama is spending time with some paper? Silly cat!" She continued to pat him as she stared at what she could see of the paper. After some deliberation, she decided she would just write a poem about Hail. No use wracking her brain when inspiration was already standing on the page, right?

She wrote, "I love my cat. His name is Hail. / He has a cute, little, white tip on his tail." She stopped and looked at her work. And just like that, she was stuck again. She chewed on her pencil. Hail lay down on her poem. They held those positions for a long time, and Gertrude was starting to think writing a poem was too hard when she had an idea. She jumped in her chair. Hail lifted his head and stared at her.

"No offense, Hail, but I have a better idea! I'm going to write a poem about one of the victims. I'll pretend that I knew her, that I am overcome with grief!"

She stood up. She knew she would need Facebook for her research, and her first instinct was to scurry over to Calvin and his computer, but she knew he would just give her grief about not studying for the driver's test. *I don't need Calvin. I've got my phone.* She sat back down. Hail gave her a dirty look and a flip of his tail. Gertrude dug through her walker pouch until she came up with her cell. Then she got to work.

Facebook provided her with more than enough info, but Gertrude also looked up Abby's obituary, so she could get some names of family members. She also had to look up the word "polyamorous" as that's what Abby's Facebook profile called her. As she began to read the definition, her cheeks started to feel hot. She closed the tab before finishing the definition. She had learned enough.

4

Gertrude had no idea what to wear to a poetry slam. She thought she should probably try to look a little like a gangster, as "slam" sounded pretty violent, but Calvin had said it would be a bunch of English teachers and librarians. She wasn't sure what garb could cover both bases. So she chose a long orange sleeveless dress. She didn't know it, but the dress was actually a beach coverup. She put a leather jacket on over it, but then she nearly died of heat stroke just trying to exit her bedroom. She took the leather jacket off and stuffed it back into her leather tote, where she noticed a leather studded dog collar. "Perfect!" she declared out loud and then tried it on. It fit snugly around her neck. She was getting there, but she still felt she could do better. She remembered she had some ugly lipsticks left over from her Grace Space misadventures, and she rummaged around until she found them. Then she put on a heavy coat of "plum." She smacked her lips together, looking in the mirror. "Not bad," she said, "not bad." But still, could there be more? Calvin had said something about poets wearing berets. She had one of those, right? She found her hat bin and began to dig, silently mourning the straw hat she'd lost when she'd mud-wrestled the VardSale kidnapper. "There you are!" She pulled a forest green beret out of the bin, fondly remembering when she'd found it at a Salvation Army store, and, after punching it back into shape, placed it on her head and returned to the mirror. *There. Not bad, Gert. You might just look like a poet.*

She made sure she had her poem in her walker pouch and then she headed over to Calvin's.

When he opened the door, the color immediately drained from his face. He didn't speak at first. He just stood staring. Then he was slowly overcome with mirth. A chuckle turned into a belly laugh that turned into a tip his head back and gasp for air as tears slid out of the corners of his eyes.

"Are you ready to go?" Gertrude asked. She couldn't imagine what was wrong with him.

He didn't answer at first because he was having so much trouble breathing, but finally he got ahold of himself and said, "I'm not going anywhere with you looking like that."

"What's wrong with how I look? I'm dressed like a poet!"

"You are not!" Calvin snapped. His sense of humor had apparently fled the scene.

"I am so! I looked it up on my phone," Gertrude lied. "This is what poets look like."

Calvin hesitated as if he didn't know whether to believe her. Then he said, "I don't see how that's possible."

"Oh, come on, Calvin," she said, turning toward the car. "We've got to go or we're going to be late."

Gertrude needn't have worried. The event had been advertised to start at seven, and though she and Calvin arrived right on time, they were one of the first ones there.

Parking was problematic. The event was called "Poetland Slam," but it actually took place at Alfonso's Punk Rock Club, which was in the Old Port, where parking spots are scarce. Calvin refused to pay for a parking garage, so they drove around and around looking for somewhere to land. "There!" Gertrude called out, pointing.

"That's a fire hydrant, Gertrude."

"There!" she tried again.

"That's a driveway, Gertrude."

"There!"

"Loading zone! Can't you read the signs, Gertrude?"

"Don't be mean! How about there?"

Calvin read the sign. "It says two-hour parking. Will we be in there more than two hours?"

"I can't imagine. No one can listen to more than two hours of poetry!"

"OK then." Calvin expertly parallel parked his Cadillac.

"Wow. You're good at that. You're going to have to teach me."

"I'm going to have to do no such thing. You be careful getting out. Don't bang my car door into the sidewalk."

Despite her best efforts, she banged the bottom of his door on the sidewalk. But it didn't make much noise, so she wasn't sure he even knew it happened. When he didn't mention it, she assumed that he didn't.

"What's taking so long?" he asked.

"Oh hold your ponies, I've got to get my walker." She opened the back door and retrieved her walker and then joined him at the crosswalk.

"Ready?" he asked.

"Yep. I'm loaded for bear."

"What?" he asked, but she had already headed across the street. He quickly caught her and then slowed down to her pace so that they headed side-by-side down Pearl Street until they reached the advertised address. Then they stopped. And looked up.

They were standing in front of a Chinese restaurant. To their right was a cotton candy store, and to their left an art gallery.

"Are you sure this is the right address, Gert?"

"Yes, look!"

Calvin looked. Wedged between the egg rolls and spun sugar stood a foreboding door. It read, in faded letters, Alfonso's Punk Rock Club.

"You've got to be kidding," Calvin said.

"I don't think so. Let's go."

As she opened the door, Calvin said, "What is it, a closet?"

"Nope," Gertrude said, looking in. "Stairs."

Calvin looked over her shoulders. "Oh dear. Stairs to a dungeon?" What paltry light the stairway had served only to illuminate the filthiness of the stairs. The walls were covered in graffiti-art. There was no sign of life at the bottom—only another door. "Gertrude, I'm not sure this is such a good idea. I'm legitimately frightened. Let's go get some Chinese food. You can get extra chicken wings."

"Oh don't be such a yellowbelly. Come on." Gertrude expertly swung her walker into her left hand and grabbed the rickety railing with her right. Then, down she went. And Calvin followed. It took some time, but there was no one there to rush them. When Gertrude got to the bottom, she didn't even hesitate. She just flung open the second door.

And Calvin gasped.

Gertrude stepped right in.

"Hi there!" a chipper young woman said from her seat beside the door. She sat behind a small table that held two sign-up sheets and a cash box. "Welcome to Poetland!" she said in a high-pitched voice.

"Thank you," Gertrude said. "I would like to poetry slam."

The girl smiled. "Great! You're the first to sign up." She pointed to one of the sign-up sheets.

Gertrude wrote "Hazel Walker" on the sheet.

Calvin raised an eyebrow.

Gertrude winked at him.

"What's that sheet for?" Calvin asked the chipper woman, pointing to the other one.

"That's the open mic," the chipper woman answered.

"There's an open mic?" Calvin said. He leaned closer to Gertrude, "Hazel, why don't you just do the open mic?"

"No!" Gertrude said, returning the pen to the table with an emphatic snap. "I want to slam."

Then she walked off toward the seats, so she didn't hear Calvin when he muttered, "I'm not so sure that's a verb."

Calvin looked apologetically at the chipper woman and said, "How much?"

"Three dollars each, please."

"Thank you. So, not a big turnout tonight, huh?"

She took his money. "No, don't worry. It's early."

Calvin looked at his watch. "It's already past seven."

She tittered. "Oh, I know, but these people are on poet time!"

Calvin grimaced, took his change, and headed toward Gertrude, who had plopped down in the very center of the room.

"I wasn't very far off with my dungeon comment," Calvin said when he reached her.

"I like it," Gertrude said, looking around. "It's kind of ... homey."

"Homey?" Calvin said, clearly appalled. "Only if you think prison cells are homey! I mean, what is this place? And why can't they afford lightbulbs?"

He sat down in the chair beside her. The basement room was about 800 square feet and packed full of small, lopsided tables and ripped chairs, which so far, remained empty. A few people sat at the bar that ran along the back of the room, but the room was quiet and peaceful. So when the bathroom door slammed behind them, Calvin jumped in his chair.

"Oh, will you settle down? You're as nervous as a June bride."

"I'll settle down when this is over, and we are back in my car. Speaking of which, this had better get going, or we're going to be parked for too long."

"Oh relax. Just enjoy the art." Gertrude looked at the wall.

"That's not art. It's vandalism."

"Oh bosh. It's all a matter of perspective. We're supposed to be undercover, you know, so don't make a scene."

"I'm making a scene?" Calvin cried, incredulous. "You're the one wearing a dog collar! You look like a serial killer on her way to the beach." Calvin wiggled his nose. "It smells weird in here, a mixture of old booze, vomit, and fried rice."

"Hello, Poetland!" a large man cried from the doorway he had just burst through.

The chipper woman smiled. "Hi, Ned. How are you tonight?"

"I'm excited to hear some poetry! Here, keep the change." He bent over to scribble on one of the sign-up sheets.

Calvin turned back around toward Gertrude. "Well, he looks normal enough, even if he is a little rowdy."

The man, who looked fortyish, was wearing khaki slacks and a pale-yellow polo shirt. He did, indeed, look a little run-of-the-mill, and Gertrude nervously fingered her collar.

"Greetings, my poetry friends!" The loud man declared from beside them, where he had just appeared.

Gertrude jumped. "Uh, hello."

The man stuck out his hand. "Ned Nelson, at your service. Is this your first time here?"

Gertrude didn't respond, so Calvin stuck his hand out and shook Ned's. "Yes. First time. I'm Calvin and this is Ger—"

Gertrude elbowed him, hard. "I'm Hazel," she said. "Hazel Walker."

"Right," Calvin said. "This is my friend Hazel. She wanted to see what this poetry slam thing is all about."

Ned grabbed Gertrude's hand, even though she hadn't offered it, and pumped it up and down. She yanked it from his sweaty grip. He didn't seem offended. "Aw, you're going to love it!"

Gertrude leaned away from him. He was so *loud*.

"It's such fun. Do you want to be a judge?"

Calvin guffawed. "I don't think she's qualified to be a judge. And in any case, she wants to actually compete."

"Aw! That's great!" Ned slapped Gertrude on the back.

"Please stop touching me," she said.

Again, Ned was unfazed. "You'll do great. Don't be nervous or anything."

"I'm not nervous."

Ned didn't seem to hear her. "This is such a supportive community, and we love to welcome new poets. You folks live in Portland?"

"No, Mattawooptock," Gertrude said.

"Matta-what? Where the heck is that?" Ned laughed. He sounded a little like a seal with a megaphone.

"It's about two hours north of here," Calvin said.

"Holy smokes! What brings you guys all the way down to the city?"

"Abby Livingstone was my cousin," Gertrude said. Calvin looked at her in surprise. "I am grieving her deeply. I thought coming here might make me feel close to her."

"Ah, I see," Ned said, his mood shifting. "Well I am sorry for your loss. Abby was a nice girl."

"You knew her?" Gertrude said. She felt her heart rate pick up.

"Not well," Ned said, "but I listened to her poems every week. That makes you know a person fairly well."

"Was she good at poetry?" Gertrude asked.

Ned nodded. "She was real good. She had just started to win, was on a roll really. Of course, her, uh, *presentation* helped." Ned raised his eyebrows at Gertrude as if to say, *if you know what I mean.*

"I have no idea what you mean," Gertrude said. "Presentation?"

Ned got a little red. "Well, I didn't mean to sound judgmental. To each their own, right? But Abby was right out

27

there about sexuality. All her poems were about sex. And she was sexy. I mean, her poems were great, but sex gets good scores too."

"I see," Gertrude said thoughtfully, her lips pursed.

"I'm going to go get a drink," Ned announced. "I'll be back."

"Well," Calvin said when Ned was out of earshot, "that might complicate things."

"Yep," Gertrude agreed. "Sounds like my cousin was quite a rig."

5

Ned took his time returning to his seat beside Gertrude. As he made his way around the room, greeting each and every soul, his path easy to track by the boom of his voice, the room slowly filled with people, and Calvin looked more and more nervous.

"Oh my word, Gertrude. I don't know if I can take this."

"Take what?" Gertrude asked, even though she had a good idea what he meant.

"These people. Why are they all so ... so ... so *strange*?"

"I told you—this is what poets look like."

"You were right," Calvin said. "You do look like you fit in." He looked her up and down and then amended, "Sort of."

While there were several people who looked like Calvin and Ned, there were also dozens who looked a smidge less traditional. There seemed to be hair of every shade—from turquoise to fire engine red to rainbow striped.

"And all the tattoos and piercings aren't even the worst part," Calvin whispered. "Why do these young women have to be so scantily clad?"

"Shh," Gertrude said absentmindedly. "Someone will hear you."

"Is this seat taken?" a young woman with a shaved head asked.

"Yes, sorry," Gertrude said, though she couldn't imagine why she was saving a seat for Ned.

"Why was she bald?" Calvin asked.

Gertrude looked at him, wide-eyed. "That will be *enough* out of you, Calvin! This is how these people choose to express themselves, and it has nothing to do with you! Now, will you please untangle your britches and help me look for clues. *Quietly*."

Calvin looked shocked at Gertrude's reprimand, but he did pipe down.

Just in time too, as a woman took the stage. The stage was empty save for a single microphone, which the woman grabbed confidently. She was wearing jeans and a Star Trek T-shirt. Her hair was brown. Nary a piercing or tattoo in sight.

Gertrude felt a little guilty about being so harsh with Calvin, so she leaned toward him and said, "See? She's not so bad."

He grunted.

"Welcome, everyone," the woman said with moderate enthusiasm. "We're glad you're here. My name is Beth, and I will be your host for the evening. As most of you know, our community has been punched in the gut this week, and we are hurting. We have lost someone very special, and so I would like to dedicate this evening to Abby Livingstone. Let's celebrate her life with our art. Now, without further mayhem, let's get started with the open mic, so here's the time I say things like, please turn off your phones, and please keep your poems to under five minutes. That means five minutes per poet, not five minutes per poem, OK? We have to be out of here by one, so I have to be strict about that. Don't make me chase you off the stage."

Calvin looked at Gertrude wide-eyed.

"Maybe you should go move the car," Gertrude said.

"Now, we are at capacity," Beth continued, "so if you need to slip out for anything, to make a phone call or have a smoke, realize that you're probably going to lose your seat. We've got people waiting outside, just hoping that one of you leaves so they can slip in."

Calvin looked at Gertrude again.

She couldn't help it—she found his bewilderment hysterical.

"OK, are we ready for some poetry, Poetland?" Beth asked, her voice rising to a crescendo.

The crowd, impressive now that it was five past eight, gave her a rousing response that sounded like a collective roar.

Gertrude shuddered.

"OK then, without further empty banter, let me introduce you to tonight's first poet ... Ned!"

Gertrude shuddered again.

Ned, who still hadn't reclaimed his seat beside Gertrude, made his way from the bar to the stage.

He'd only read three lines when Gertrude looked at Calvin. "This doesn't even rhyme!"

Calvin rolled his eyes. "Poems don't have to rhyme, Gertrude. Didn't you go to school?"

Gertrude gave him an indignant glare, which he did not see.

Next up to the stage was the chipper woman, whose name, it turned out, wasn't chipper woman, but Jade. She read a poem about how much she loves her sister. Gertrude looked at Calvin to see how he was faring. He was staring straight ahead, expressionless, with his arms folded across his chest. He looked like someone in a colonoscopy waiting room.

The crowd clapped enthusiastically for Jade, and she stepped down from the stage looking quite satisfied. Beth took the stage again. "I'd like to take this time to remind you to drink from the bar, so that Alfonso will continue to let us use his space. OK, next up is Bubbles!"

Gertrude snickered. *Bubbles?* A person of indeterminate gender took the stage and read a poem about living life without gender.

Calvin put his hands on his legs and began to stand up as he said, "That's it. I'll wait in the car."

Gertrude reached up, grabbed his sleeve, and yanked him back into his chair. "Enough! This will be good for you. Not everyone is like you, Calvin! Get over it! We are here to catch a murderer. Now, pay attention!"

Bubbles was still performing as Gertrude was scolding Calvin, and a woman in the row in front of them turned around to glare at the disruption.

"Sorry," Gertrude whispered.

The woman turned back toward the front.

"We don't even know there's been a murder," Calvin mumbled.

The woman turned around to glare again.

"Sorry, sorry," Calvin said, holding one hand up apologetically.

The woman turned front again.

"There has been," Gertrude whispered. "Trust me."

Bubbles finished, was lauded with cheers and whistles and exactly two claps from Calvin, and then left the stage. As Beth headed toward the mic again, Ned plopped into the seat beside Gertrude.

"How's it going?" he asked, slurring just a smidge. Then, without letting her answer, he added, "How're you liking it?"

Beth welcomed the next poet to the stage. King William. Calvin rolled his eyes but stayed quiet. King William had giant holes in his earlobes and his hair was gathered into giant spikes that jutted out from his head at all angles. And he read an elegant villanelle about his grandmother. As he read, someone began snapping his fingers. Then someone else followed suit.

Calvin muttered, "Is that like a poet's version of applause?"

Gertrude looked around, noting the pleased expressions on the snappers' faces. "I believe so."

She'd lost count of how many poets had read when her right leg started to fall asleep. She slyly removed her phone from her walker pouch so she could check the time. It was 9:30. She looked at Calvin. He appeared to be in an open-eye coma. She looked at Ned, who returned her gaze. His eyes were glassy, and he gave her a lopsided grin. "How long does this last?" she whispered.

He shrugged. "Dunno. Long's it takes, I s'pose."

Gertrude wanted to slap him. "Well, when does the slam start?"

Ned leaned away from her so he could dig into his pocket. He pulled out his phone and looked at it. "Slam usually starts about 11."

You needed your phone for that? She turned toward the front, wondering if this whole thing had been a horrible error.

Just then, Beth said, "We've only got five more poets in the open, and then we'll get ready for the slam!"

Calvin looked at Gertrude then, and it was the dirtiest look he'd ever given her, and that's saying something. "I wish I were dead," he said.

"You should write a poem about that," she said and returned her eyes to the stage as she tried to massage some feeling back into her right leg.

6

It was time for the slam. While Beth wandered around the room with marker boards looking for judges, and everyone else stood, stretched, and refilled their drinks, Gertrude followed the directive to head toward a corner of the room for the "draw." She had no idea what this meant. She pictured two gunslingers from one of Calvin's westerns squaring off in a dusty street.

This draw, as it turned out, had nothing to do with pistols. Eight competitors crowded around a young man holding a hat. He quickly rattled through the rules, but Gertrude had already read most of them online: no props, must be original work, three-minute time limit.

Each poet reached into the hat and drew a small piece of crumpled paper.

With dismay, she watched one of the poets, a hairy man with lots of tattoos, eat his piece of paper. With even more dismay, she realized that none of the other poets found this odd. *And people say I'm peculiar.*

When it was Gertrude's turn to reach into the hat, she was overcome by an urge to grab all of the remaining scraps of paper, but she resisted and limited herself to one. Unfolding the paper revealed the number 1.

Pushing down on the walker with her left hand, she shot her right fist into the air, gave a little hop, and shouted, "Yippee!"

The other poets all stared at her as if she had lizards crawling out of her ears.

"What?" she asked.

"Oh nothing," a tall young woman with shiny silver hair said. "It's just, most people don't want to go first. We all try *not* to draw the one. That's cool, though. Glad you're good with it."

"I am," Gertrude said defensively. "Good with it," she added. She folded the paper back up and slipped it into her pocket. Then she said, "You're awfully young for silver hair, aren't you?"

The girl just smiled tolerantly.

Gertrude returned to her seat to find Calvin had gotten himself a glass of wine.

"Calvin!" she accused. "You have to drive me home!"

"Gertrude, I believe we're going to be here for several more hours. I'll be fine. I thought maybe a glass of wine would help me to stop agonizing about the giant parking ticket on my windshield right now."

"Oh don't worry. I'll help you pay it."

"Sure you will," he said sarcastically.

"I appreciate your confidence," Gertrude said sincerely.

Beth took the stage again. "OK, Poetland," she cried enthusiastically. "We are going to have ourselves a poetry slam!"

The crowd burst into cheers and whistles.

Gertrude's belly did a small flip.

Beth continued, "This is a qualifying slam, which means tonight's winner will be eligible to compete in the indie semifinals, which will eventually lead us to find out who will represent us at the Individual World Poetry Slam this October in Austin, Texas!

More hoots, claps, stomps, and whistles.

"Is there another Austin?" Calvin muttered sarcastically, and rhetorically.

"How should I know?" Gertrude said.

Beth introduced the judges and then she read a short history of poetry slam from her clipboard, "Poetry slam was invented in the 1980s by a Chicago construction worker named Marc Smith—"

The crowd interrupted her with a wildly loud, unified cry of "So what?!" that made Calvin literally jump in his chair.

He looked at Gertrude wide-eyed. Then he swore. "What was that all about?"

"I don't know. Watch your mouth."

"You've got to be kidding. These so-called poets have been cursing up a storm."

Gertrude rolled her eyes. "Cursing isn't contagious, Calvin. Don't blame them."

It turned out that Gertrude wasn't really the first poet. First, there was a "calibration poet," a poet whose poem was to calibrate the judges' scoring. A young woman got up and recited a poem from memory. An alarm went off in Gertrude's head. She looked at Calvin.

"What?" Calvin asked.

"Why isn't she reading her poem?"

"What?" Calvin repeated.

Gertrude leaned closer to him. "She has her poem *memorized! I don't have my poem memorized!*" She felt something close to panic.

"Don't worry," Calvin said dismissively. "You'll be fine."

"Oh, you just don't care a hoot!" Gertrude cried.

The woman in front of them turned to deliver another glare.

The scores went up. Beth read them aloud. They ranged from 5.2 to 8.1. Gertrude thought she might be sick.

"OK, the first poet of the slam is Hazel Walker!" Beth announced with what struck Gertrude as excessive energy.

Gertrude didn't move. She couldn't move.

Calvin nudged her with an elbow.

"I can't," Gertrude said, her voice quivering.

Calvin leaned closer. "Gertrude, you have done far more difficult things than this. You are the spunkiest woman I've ever known. Now get up there. I drove to Portland for this."

Gertrude found Calvin's words far more confounding than the situation at hand, and her legs stood up on their own. Still looking at Calvin, she slowly made her way to the stage. Someone stepped up to help her onto the stage, but she avoided his assistance. "I can do it. I'm not old," she said. She climbed onto the stage and turned to face the crowd, who stared at her expectantly. The crowd looked far bigger from up there than it had from her seat. She gulped and then reached into her walker pouch. "I've got my poem in here somewhere," she said, jumping when her own voice boomed back to her from the house speakers. She looked at the microphone as if only just then realizing it was there.

"Your time has started," someone called out from the crowd.

"Ya, ya," Gertrude said, less startled this time by the volume of her own voice. She was starting to like having a microphone. She found her poem, unfolded it, and then stepped closer to the mic. Her walker bumped into the mic stand, causing a loud boom.

Several people in the audience snickered. Most people just stared at her, waiting patiently.

She leaned over her walker, so her mouth was close to the mic. Then she cleared her throat. "This is my poem," she said. Then she began to read.

7

A bby Livingstone was a living stone.
 Ordinary like most, but she shone
Like a beam of sunlight
Who shatters a dark night.
She was not skimpy with her love
And spread peace like a dove.
Smarter than a whip on Tuesday,
Her soul was like the Milky Way.
She was my blood.
Now my tears flood.
She was just a spring chicken.
Goodbye, my Abby Livingstone.

Gertrude looked up from her poem. The crowd stared at her. "I'm done," she said. They responded with clapping, but it was a somber applause. Still, it was applause, and it felt pretty good. Gertrude made her way back to her seat and gratefully collapsed into it.

Calvin caught her eye. "Not bad, Gert. Count me impressed." He nodded and patted her on the knee.

Her stomach did another flip.

Ned joined in. "Yeah, that was pretty great!"

"Thanks," Gertrude said.

Someone from the row behind leaned forward, squeezed her shoulder, and whispered, "That was beautiful. Thank you for sharing your heart."

Gertrude nodded, only feeling a little guilty for the gigantic lie she had just told from the stage. All of this praise was unprecedented for Gertrude, and it felt pretty good, but nothing was as gratifying as that little pat Calvin had given Gertrude's knee. This realization significantly confused Gertrude.

Next up to the stage was Ashes LaFlamme, the silver-haired, and now, Gertrude learned, silver-tongued, girl who had spoken to her during the draw. Ashes was amazing, and Gertrude felt a little mesmerized. For starters, she was physically beautiful, extra curvy in some places, but seeming to be proud of it. She had a giant, almost hypnotic smile. And she was just so *shiny*. Her clothes were shiny; her jewelry was shiny; and her silver hair reflected the spotlight. And she was ridiculously confident, looking like she felt right at home there in the limelight.

Gertrude leaned toward Ned. "I take it she's been at this a while?"

"A-huh," Ned confirmed. "She's kind of famous. Goes to nationals every year. Features all over the country. That's why she hasn't qualified yet because she's been touring. She's a hotshot."

Gertrude nodded as if she understood, which she almost did.

Ashes's poem was alternately hilarious and horrifying, and Gertrude felt as if she was on an emotional seesaw.

The judges gave Ashes a 27.7, and Gertrude realized she had been in such a tizzy, she hadn't heard her own scores. She leaned toward Calvin, "What was my score?"

He shrugged. "Not sure. Not that high."

"Gee, thanks."

Calvin smirked.

It was the closest thing Gertrude had seen to a smile on his face in several hours.

After Ashes sashayed off the stage, a woman named "Zest" took the stage.

Calvin rolled his eyes at the announcement of her name. "Her name's probably really Jane," he whispered. Then he added, "At least this one's a grown-up. She may even be your age, Gertrude."

Gertrude chose to ignore that bait.

Zest recited an angry poem about her mother. Halfway through the poem, Gertrude realized she was going to have trouble remembering all these crazy names, and she fished around in her pouch for a notebook. Then she began to take notes. Ned kept trying to sneak a peek, but she was onto him, and kept her scribbles hidden from his prying eyes.

Zest stomped off the stage and then looked offended by her score of 25.

The fourth poet was a man named Blaine.

"That might actually be his real name," Calvin said.

Gertrude recognized him as the one who had eaten his number. Blaine was even louder than Ned, though he seemed to have saved all his volume for the stage. He recited a poem about teaching high school English, and he managed to scream the entire poem into the microphone, spit flying out of his mouth with such force that Gertrude thanked God she hadn't sat in the front row.

"I can't believe they let a man with that many tattoos teach high school," Calvin said. She could barely hear him over Blaine's production.

"Forget the tattoos, why is he so *mad*?"

But apparently, the judges liked loud and furious because Blaine got himself a 28 even. Gertrude snuck a look at Ashes. She didn't look happy.

The next poet only said three words before Gertrude felt her cheeks blushing. Gertrude had never seen a naughty movie, but she thought that they must sound a lot like this girl's poem. Rose Waters was a redheaded sexpot. Gertrude snuck a look at Calvin and did not appreciate his suddenly intensified interest in poetry.

Gertrude was glad when Rose left the stage, but the judges apparently wanted more of her because they gave her a 27.8. Gertrude glanced at Ashes, who was smiling and clapping, but Gertrude could tell that her smile was a big, fat fib.

Calvin leaned toward Gertrude. "I'll admit. This is far less violent than I thought it would be. They call it a *slam*. I expected some, I don't know, *slam*ming or something."

The sixth poet genuinely frightened Gertrude. He looked like he might actually slam someone into something. Thor had more tattooed skin than untattooed skin. He was bald, and his scalp was tattooed too. He was also a shouter, but his poem made far less sense than the English teacher's had. Gertrude would readily admit that she didn't know much about poetry, but she thought maybe she knew enough to guess that this guy's poem was pretty bad. She thought the poem was about being drunk, but she wasn't prepared to testify to that in court. The judges were either drunk and could identify, they understood his poem better than Gertrude had, or both. They gave him a 27.9.

Gertrude was ready for the slam to be over, and it was still only the first round. Not only was she completely sick of poetry, but she also wanted to talk to some of these people, poke around, ask some probing questions. She was sick of being tied to her chair.

The next poet didn't help much. Sinclair's poem didn't even make sense, and he used too many big words. Gertrude found him a bit uppity for her taste. The judges liked his poem, though, and gave him a 28. Gertrude looked at Ashes, whom she decided she was silently cheering for, but Ashes was on her way to the bar.

Finally, the last poet in the first round was a young man named Alec. His youthfully handsome face was crowned with a tall rainbow mohawk. That was all Gertrude could look at. As he nodded his head passionately at his own words, the mohawk sliced back and forth through the air, creating quite a spectacle. His poem was about going to rehab for a drug addiction.

"That's it," Gertrude whispered, excitedly. "He's our guy."

"Why?" Calvin muttered. "Because he's a drug addict?"

"No! Because he's lying!"

Calvin looked at her, his eyebrows raised haughtily. "Gertrude, these people are poets. They're all liars."

8

Rose the sexpot, Blaine the angry English teacher, Sinclair the snob, and Alec the rainbow-haired murderer advanced to the second round. The rest were knocked out. Gertrude learned that she had come in last with a measly 19.2. She stood.

"Where are you going?" Calvin asked, alarmed.

"To the bar," Gertrude announced.

Ashes was slumped on a barstool. Gertrude turned back to the bar and, backing up, wedged herself between Ashes's barstool and the one beside her, which was also occupied. Each of Gertrude's hips rubbed on someone's leg. Ashes looked up and smiled at her, not seeming to mind the physical contact. The man gave Gertrude a dirty look and slid over a few inches but did not vacate his spot.

"You're my favorite," Gertrude announced to Ashes.

"Aw!" Ashes said. "Thanks so much." She seemed genuinely appreciative, but Gertrude also sensed that she was used to receiving praise.

"I thought your poem was the best. I don't know why you didn't get to the second round."

Ashes used a few expletives to express her idea that the judges were to blame.

Gertrude nodded, trying to look empathic, a state Gertrude was entirely unfamiliar with.

Ashes took a long swallow of her beer. "You were great too," she said, without looking at Gertrude. She just stared straight ahead at the mirror behind the bar. "Abby was a relative of yours?"

"Yes," Gertrude said quickly, maybe a little too quickly. "Cousin."

Ashes nodded. Then she looked at Gertrude suddenly, as if snapping to attention. "I'm sorry for your loss. I'm also sorry that I'm not being very sociable right now. I'm usually friendlier. I just really don't like losing." She swore again. And again.

"You have a potty mouth," Gertrude remarked.

Ashes laughed. She took another drink. "Thank you," she said.

"For calling you a potty mouth?"

"For making me laugh."

"Did you know Abby?"

Ashes nodded. "Of course. She was a sweet girl. She was up and coming and all that." Ashes looked at Gertrude. "Again, sorry, don't mean to sound so cynical. Just having a bad night. I'm a little overtired from touring, and I really didn't expect to come back to my home venue and then get knocked out by these ..." She paused. "These poets," she finished reluctantly. "Not that they're not good poets," she self-corrected. "They're just not really nationals material."

The bartender approached. "Ashes, you might want to keep your voice down. Probably don't want to burn any more bridges if you know what I mean."

Ashes shrugged.

"How long had you known Abby?" Gertrude whispered.

"Just a few months. She hasn't, or *hadn't* I should say, been slamming long, and I'm not here every week because of all the touring I do."

"She'd been winning, though, right?"

"I guess so," Ashes said. "She qualified last week. Not that that's a huge deal. Twelve poets qualify."

"Have you qualified?"

Ashes shook her head. "Not yet because I've been—"

"Touring," Gertrude interrupted. "Yeah, you mentioned that. When did you get home?"

Ashes raised an eyebrow. "Last week. Why?"

"Oh, just making conversation," Gertrude said. "When, specifically, last week?"

Ashes stared at her for a few seconds. Then she said, "Why are you asking?"

"Oh, I'm just a regular old Chatty Cathy."

"Don't you mean Chatty Patty?"

Gertrude scowled. "Who's Patty? No, I mean what I said. Now when did you say you got home?"

"I got home July 1st, but I really don't understand why you need to know, and Chatty Patty was a parrot. I used to have one." She took another swig.

"So, were you here last week?"

Ashes nodded, looking at the mirror.

"And you didn't win that week either."

She looked at Gertrude out of the corner of her eye. "You're not big on tact, are you?"

"I get that a lot."

"No. I didn't win. Abby did."

"Ah, I see. So you must have been pretty mad."

"Nah. Not really. She earned it. Like I said, she was a good poet."

"You never said that."

"No? Well I meant to."

The bartender returned. "I know you ladies are oblivious, but you're getting lots of dirty looks. People are trying to hear the poems."

"We're whispering!" Gertrude said.

"Right, well, maybe you should stop whispering and just shut up," he said and slunk off.

"How rude!" Gertrude cried.

"Nah," Ashes said. "He's all right." She swore again, but affectionately this time.

"Did you know John Crane?" Gertrude asked.

Ashes's head snapped up. "No, why?"

Gertrude furrowed her brow. Ashes was lying.

Ashes must have sensed Gertrude's suspicions because she altered her position. "Well, I know *of* him. I mean, I knew who he was. I talked to him a few times, but I didn't really know him. Why do you ask? He your cousin too?"

"No. But he was a friend of Abby's."

Ashes held the glass up to her lips, but she didn't drink. "I didn't know that," she said thoughtfully.

"How did you know him?"

"Oh, just from being around. It's a small town."

"No, it's not. Did you ever see him here?"

"Nope." She took a swig and then put the glass down. "You know what? Enough melancholy. What about you? What are your plans? Are you just trying this thing out or what?"

"What thing?" For a second, Gertrude thought she meant gumshoeing.

"Slam."

"Oh, *that* thing. Yes. Definitely. I have always wanted to be a poetry slam person. I love poetry." Sometimes, when Gertrude got going with a lie, the lie took over and ran away, dragging her along with it. "I want to go to nationals. I thought I would win tonight. But I think that I didn't win because I didn't have my poem memorized."

Ashes nodded, her face void of emotion. "You know what?" She stood up and reached over the bar and, after a few seconds of groping around, came up with a pen. Then she began to scribble on her napkin. "Here's my phone number. Call me with any questions, or anything. I want to help you. I do a lot of coaching for other poets. In fact, I've coached dozens of poets to the national stage. I usually charge, but I like you, so we could do a few coaching sessions for free, if you want. And here's my website. You might learn a lot just from watching my YouTube channel." She handed the napkin to Gertrude.

As Gertrude took it, the crowd erupted in applause, and for one silly second, Gertrude thought they were applauding her taking of the napkin. But then she realized that Sexy Rose had just finished another poem. The judges gave her a 30, a perfect score.

Ashes groaned audibly. "Well, I guess *she's* qualified." She waved to the bartender to bring her another beer.

9

As Beth announced Rose's victory, the room erupted into activity. As everyone stood and began to mill about, Gertrude looked around wildly for someone to interrogate. She'd been waiting for this moment for so long, but now she wasn't sure where to go first.

It was decided for her. A young man approached her quickly and said, "May I give you a hug?"

Baffled, Gertrude accidentally nodded assent.

He threw his arms around Gertrude and squeezed her.

Gertrude tolerated this for as long as she could, which was about two seconds, before pushing the hugger away.

The hugger didn't seem offended. He stepped back and gave her a giant smile before announcing, "My name is Bae, and I just *loved* your poem."

"Thank you?" Gertrude said because she didn't know what else to say.

"So, how long have you been writing?"

Gertrude was unsettled by this person's friendliness. "A while, I guess. Did you know Abby Livingstone?"

Bae's face fell into what looked like sincere sadness. "I did. She's been coming here for months. I really liked her. She was a sweet human being." Bae placed a hand on Gertrude's left hand, which was clutching her walker.

Gertrude yanked her hand away. "Did you know John Crane?"

"No, I didn't. Who's he?"

"He was a friend of Abby's. He was here last week. Now he's dead."

"Wow. That's so very, very sad."

Gertrude marveled at how earnest Bae seemed. As if he genuinely cared. About everything. In the whole world. All the time.

"Being so kind must be exhausting," Gertrude said.

Bae smiled. "Did you know John too?"

Gertrude shook her head. "Did Abby have any enemies?"

Bae's eyes grew wider. "I don't know, but she didn't have any here. We are all one big family. Sure, some of us compete—"

"Do you?" Gertrude interrupted.

"Do I what?"

"Compete?"

"I do."

"You didn't tonight."

"I'm already qualified," Bae explained.

"Oh. Congratulations then. Are you better than Ashes?"

Bae smiled broadly. "Ah, another Ashes fan, huh? Well I don't know. We have very different styles, and I'm not sure anyone is better than Ashes—"

"I heard my name," Ashes interrupted, coming alongside Gertrude.

"We were just singing your praises," Bae said. "Have I given you a hug yet tonight?"

"You sure haven't." Ashes spread her arms wide and then wrapped Bae up in them. They stood like that, swaying side to side, for a very long time.

Gertrude wasn't sure what to do with herself. She wasn't sure if she'd ever felt so awkward.

Finally, Ashes let go. "I love you," she said.

"I love you too," Bae said.

They were both positively glowing.

Bae turned his attention to Gertrude. "See? As I was saying, we are a family here. We love and support one another. No one has any enemies. And I'm so glad you've come tonight, Hazel. I hope you will come again?"

Gertrude nodded.

Bae gave her hand another pat. "You take good care now."

Gertrude looked at Ashes. "So I guess he's qualified. Sexy Rose is qualified. Sounds like you're going to have quite a bit of competition, that is, if you qualify."

"I'll qualify," Ashes said quickly. "It gets easier to qualify as the weeks go by, as there are fewer serious competitors. And

I'll win the whole thing too. Don't worry. I'm saving my big guns for the finals."

Gertrude had no idea what that meant, and it showed on her face.

Ashes explained, "We can't repeat poems. So whatever we use to qualify with, we can't use in the semis or finals. So, I've been throwing my weaker poems."

Gertrude's eyebrows flew up. "*That* was a weak poem? I thought it was great!"

"You just wait," Ashes said. "Like I said, you should check me out on YouTube ..."

Gertrude saw Beth walk by and left Ashes mid-sentence to follow her.

"Hiya, Beth!" Beth stopped walking and turned toward Gertrude, but she didn't look happy about it. "I'm Hazel. Just wanted to introduce myself."

"Nice to meet you, Hazel. I'm glad you came tonight." She turned to walk away.

"Wait!" Gertrude cried.

Beth grudgingly turned around.

"Do you know if my cousin Abby had any enemies?"

Beth frowned. "No, I don't know. Why?"

"Just wondering. Did you know John Crane?"

Beth sighed and leveled an unpleasant stare at Gertrude. "No. Now, if you'll excuse me, I'm kind of—"

"He was here last week, but I can't find anyone who knew him. Don't you think that's a bit strange?"

"No, not at all. Lots of people come through our doors. I couldn't possibly know them all. Why are you speaking of him in the past tense? Did he die?"

Gertrude nodded. She leaned toward Beth. "*Suspiciously*," she whispered.

Beth nodded thoughtfully. "Well, I'm sorry to hear that. But I doubt it has anything to do with me, or this venue, no matter how suspicious it was." She paused. "Do you know if he knew Abby?"

Gertrude nodded. "They were tight." She held up two curled-together fingers to illustrate. "Thick as thieves." Gertrude really had no idea if they even knew each other, but she figured there was a good chance.

"Huh," Beth said. "Well, maybe he just came to watch her perform then. In any case, I'm sorry for your loss, but I really need to get going. So if you'll excuse me."

Gertrude didn't want to excuse her, but she couldn't think of anything else to ask.

Calvin appeared at her side. "I want to go home."

"Hang on," Gertrude said. "I want to talk to the bartender."

Calvin sighed disgustedly, but he said, "Be quick about it."

Gertrude trotted to the bar.

"Excuse me," she called out to the barkeep.

"Bar's closed," he answered without looking at her.

"I know that," she snapped, even though she hadn't. "I need to ask you a question."

The bartender looked at her. "What?"

"Did you know John Crane?"

He shrugged. "I don't know names. Only faces. You got a picture?"

Gertrude stomped a foot in anger and glared at Calvin. "We should have brought a picture!"

"Can't you find one on Facebook?" Calvin suggested.

"Yes!" Gertrude cried and reached into her walker pouch for her phone.

"You're not going to get any signal in here," the bartender said.

"Right. Because we're in a dungeon," Calvin said.

"Come on, Calvin, we've got to get outside!" She looked at the bartender. "Be right back with a picture!"

The bartender did not respond.

Gertrude hurried to the door but then slowed down significantly on the stairs. By the time she reached the top, her back hurt, and she was huffing and puffing.

Once they got to the sidewalk, she pulled her phone out and began stabbing at the screen. Within seconds, John Crane was smiling back at her.

She hurried back to the door, but a burly bouncer blocked her path. "Sorry, closed," he said.

"I know that," Gertrude snapped. "I just need to go show the bartender something."

"Closed."

"He's expecting me."

"Still closed."

"It's a matter of life and death!" Gertrude screeched. She'd never been so frustrated in her whole life.

"Closed."

Gertrude reared back away from her walker, in order to gather momentum, and then threw her upper body forward in an effort to push the bouncer out of the way. Both her hands landed on his chest, but he did not budge. She bounced off him and nearly toppled backward.

"Oh rackafratz!" Gertrude cried in sheer fury. "Come on, Calvin! Let's go!"

"Thank God," Calvin muttered and followed her up the street. "The car's that way," he said, after a few paces.

"I know. I'm looking for a back door."

"Gertrude, no!"

"Yes, Calvin! I need to show this picture to that meanieface bartender!"

"Gertrude, you're going to get us arrested. And if I'm in there with you, who's going to bail you out? Besides, it's like ten hours past my bedtime."

Gertrude kept walking.

"Gertrude, stop! We can show him next week."

She froze. "Really?"

"Yes, really."

She looked at him. "You'll drive me back down here next Monday?"

Calvin faltered, seeming to realize his error. "I guess so."

"All right," Gertrude assented.

"All right. Let's go."

Calvin led her to the car.

"See!" she cried, triumphant. "You didn't even get a parking ticket! That's because God helps those who fight crime!"

"Well, I'll be."

Gertrude looked at the sign again and noticed something different. "Calvin."

"What?"

"We didn't read the fine print. It's only two-hour parking until six."

"Great. Tell my new ulcer that."

10

Gertrude woke up on Tuesday morning and knew that she should start studying for her driver's test. So, she decided to go to church and see if her friend Pete had dug up any intel on Tiny's food stamp card.

She hoped Norman would be driving the CAP bus, but it was Andrea.

"Good morning, Gertrude!" Andrea practically sang.

Gertrude was baffled. Andrea was usually a grump. "Good morning," she said, pulling the walker into the van behind her.

"Little Prince Charming is just so wonderful! He really is a charmer! I just love him so much. Thank you, Gertrude. I mean it."

"You're welcome," Gertrude said, shifting in her seat uncomfortably. "Open Door Church."

"On a Tuesday?"

"Yep. I'm working."

"Working? I didn't know you worked. What do you do?"

Gertrude scowled. "You don't know I work? Where you been? I've been all over the news! Don't you watch television—"

"I'm more of a reader—"

"As I was saying," Gertrude continued, miffed at the interruption, "I'm a gumshoe."

"Ah, I see," Andrea said thoughtfully. "Did you know the term 'gumshoe' originally referred to a thief?"

"I'm not a thief!" Gertrude cried. *Though, I might kife an occasional salt and pepper shaker set. But that's not stealing. Not really.*

"I know you're not a thief, Gertrude. I was just talking about the word. But it came to mean detective because it referred to the rubber soles of shoes, which allowed people to be stealthy."

"I don't care."

"So you're like a private detective?"

Gertrude wished Andrea would go back to not liking her. Give a woman a kitten, and the whole dynamic changes. "Yes. I am private. But I'm not licensed."

"Why's that?"

"I'm not going to pay someone to give me a license that says I can do what I already know I can do. There's nothing to gumshoeing really. You just got to follow the clues."

"And the clues are leading you to your church?" Andrea pulled into the church parking lot.

"Yep," Gertrude said. She flung open the door and slid out of the van. "Thanks for the ride."

"You bet!" Andrea called. "Call me when you're done!"

Gertrude slammed the door and then headed across the parking lot, pausing only once to wipe sweat from her forehead. It was going to be a scorcher. She opened the front door of the church and wished for the thousandth time that they had air conditioning. She poked her head into the office, hoping Pete would be in there. He was. "Hiya, Pete! What've you got for me?"

"Shut the door," Pete said.

Tiny sat in a chair in the corner.

"Hiya, Tiny." Gertrude shut the door. "Where's our fearless church secretary?"

"She's in the salon," Pete said. (The church's secretary doubled as a cosmetologist who volunteered in the church beauty salon.) "So"—Pete leaned back in his chair and put his hands behind his head—"I think I know who took the card, but I can't prove it."

"Don't need to prove it," Gertrude said. "Just need the card back. I doubt Tiny here wants to go through the rigmarole of getting the cops involved."

Tiny shook his head.

"Well, we think Rudolf took it. Someone else caught him trying to steal theirs—"

"The man's name is Rudolf?"

"Guess so. Anyway, I'm pretty sure he took it. Sells his own for drug money. But he doesn't have it anymore, which means, we have to figure out who he sold it too."

"All right." Gertrude waited, hoping there was more.

There was. "I only know of two people who buy food stamp cards. I checked with one of them, but she swore up and down she didn't have it. I don't want to check with the other one because she's kind of stuck up, and, well, I don't want to be a rat. If I spook her, and she stops giving the guys money for the cards, they'll hate me forever."

"I'll ask her. I don't care if the guys hate me forever. I don't live here anymore. Who is she?"

"The CAP bus driver. The one who's always on her high horse."

"You're joshing me."

"No, ma'am."

"Don't call me ma'am." Gertrude turned and headed back the way she'd come. "I'll have your card back in two shakes of a lamb's tail, Tiny."

Tiny looked confused.

"Thanks, Pete," Gertrude added on her way out the door. She stepped out into the sunlight and dialed the number.

Andrea was back in less than a minute.

"That was quick," Andrea said. "Where to?"

Gertrude slammed the van door. "Nowhere. Andrea, we need to have ourselves a little chitchat."

"OK." Andrea took her hand off the shifter and looked at her in the rearview.

Gertrude put a hand on her shoulder. "Now, you need to know that you're not in any trouble."

"OK," Andrea said tentatively.

"I need one of the food stamp cards back."

"What are you talking about?"

Gertrude noted that she was a skilled fibber. "Andrea, don't. I know you buy them, and I really don't care. But you accidentally bought one that wasn't for sale. And I need it back."

Andrea's face flushed maroon. Her eyes fell away from the mirror. "I don't even do it for myself. I do it for my grandkids. I wouldn't do something like that. I'm a law-abiding citizen—"

"I said I don't care."

"My daughter is a single mom, and she's having a real tough time. The guys here get way more than they can use. It's not like I'm really stealing—"

"Andrea, I just want the card."

Andrea reached onto the floor. For a second, Gertrude flashed back to the time she'd been kidnapped by a criminal in a van, and absurdly thought Andrea was reaching for a gun. But she wasn't. She sat up, clutching only a purse.

"You're not going to tell anyone?" she asked.

"Nope."

Andrea began to flip through some cards. "Which one?"

"Tiny's."

Andrea looked at her in the rearview. "Tiny? I don't have a card that says Tiny. What's his real name?"

"I have no idea. Just give me the stack and I'll look at the pictures."

Andrea wordlessly held them back over her shoulder.

Gertrude took them. "Jumping hot beans! How many of these do you have?"

"The shelter feeds them. They'd rather have cash than groceries."

Tiny's face graced the third card in the pile. "Got it." She handed the other cards back to Andrea. "Is there any money left on it?"

"Yes, lots. I never make big purchases. I try not to attract any attention."

"Alrighty. Let me scoot this back to its rightful owner. If you wait right here, I'd appreciate another ride home."

Andrea took the cards uncertainly. "Sure. I'll wait right here."

Gertrude wasn't sure if this was another fib, but she figured it wouldn't be the end of the world if Andrea took off.

Back inside the office, Gertrude handed Tiny his card.

He jumped to his feet and threw his bulky arms around Gertrude, jamming the walker into Gertrude's abdomen.

"Ow! Tiny! Get off me!"

He let go. "Thanks, Gertrude. You really are a very smart detective."

Gertrude nodded. "I know."

11

The next morning, after a big breakfast of scrambled eggs and pickles, Gertrude and her walker headed down the narrow, one-way street to Calvin's trailer. She rapped on the door.

He opened it. "Yes?"

"Good morning."

"Gertrude, what?"

"It's time to go."

"Go where?"

"To the driver's test!"

"I thought you were taking the CAP bus for this."

"Oh. Well, I could have, but now I can't. No time. Come on, get your moccasins on. I'll meet you at the car."

Calvin got Gertrude to the testing site in Skowhegan at five minutes till ten. She started to climb out of the car and then noticed he wasn't moving. "Aren't you coming in?"

"I'll just wait here. Good luck." He reclined his seat with a thump.

"You all right?" she asked.

"Yes. Just more comfortable out here. Now, shoo," he said, laying his right arm over his eyes.

So Gertrude headed into the BMV alone.

The place was deserted. Gertrude headed straight for a window, where a phlegmatic woman looked at her appointment card and then pointed to a door that said, "Testing."

Gertrude shuffled across the vacant room and opened the door. The room was full of desks, currently occupied by two young women. A man with a dour look on his face stood in the front of the room. He greeted Gertrude by glancing at the clock over the door.

"Is this where I take my driver's test?" she asked.

One of the young women snickered.

The man nodded.

"All right then." Gertrude sat down.

The man looked at the clock again and then said, "We are going to begin. You have an hour to complete the test, which should be plenty of time. If you finish the test early, bring it to the front of the room. I will grade it right there in front of you, and then I'll either give you your permit or a retest date. Starting now, you are not allowed to leave the room until you complete the test. You are also not allowed to use any electronic devices. There is no eating, drinking, smoking, or chewing gum during the ..."

Gertrude yawned. Loudly.

The proctor gave her a dirty look. Finally, he also gave her the test.

She took a deep breath and then bent over it and took a look. Most of the questions were just common sense, like yielding to pedestrians with white canes and not stopping on railroad tracks, but when she got to the questions about rotaries, she panicked. She had no idea what to do in a rotary. Couldn't she just promise to never enter one? She just chose "C" on these questions.

She was the first one done. She wasn't sure if this was good or bad, but she headed toward the front, and then tentatively handed the test to the proctor, who took it.

It took him less than a minute to grade it. Then, on top of the front page, he wrote, "100%."

Gertrude's eyes grew wide. "Are you sure?"

"Shh!" He glowered at her. Then he nodded his sureness and held her permit out to her.

She took it, and then, unable to help herself, let out a "Yippee!" as she turned toward the door.

"Shh!" he said again, but she was already leaving.

Calvin was snoring. When Gertrude slammed the door, he startled awake. He wiped his lips and then returned his seat to an upright position. "Well, that didn't take long."

"How would you know? You've been asleep! I could've been in there for hours. I could've been taken hostage and you wouldn't even have known it."

"You weren't taken hostage, and I wasn't sleeping. Now, how did it go?"

She shoved her shiny new permit in his face.

He pulled his head back so he could get a clear look. "Is that—"

"It sure is! Sure as peanuts in peanut butter."

Calvin was apparently speechless. He just kept staring at the permit as if he couldn't quite believe it was real.

"Can I drive?"

He guffawed. "You most certainly cannot."

"Well, will you drive me someplace safe where I can drive?"

Calvin started the car. "There is no place on earth where it would be safe for you to drive. And you're not driving my car. Ever."

Thirty minutes later, they were in the high school parking lot. It was empty because it was July. He turned the car off but stayed sitting in the driver's seat.

"Calvin, I promise not to crash your car. I'll drive like a turtle on Sleepytime Tea. Come on now."

Calvin nodded. Then he slowly climbed out of his Cadillac, and walked around the front of it, meeting Gertrude in front of the grill, where he handed her the keys.

She took them in one hand, gleefully, and steadied herself on the hood of the car with the other as she hustled around to the driver's side door, which still stood open. She slid into the front seat.

"I wish we had some cones or something to practice with," Calvin said.

"Nah, we don't need no cones." She started the car.

"All right. If you go more than fifteen miles per hour, this is over. Do you hear me?"

"Loud and clear." She looked at him expectantly.

"What?"

"What do I do now?"

Calvin rolled his eyes. "Now you put it in gear."

She put her hand on the shifter. "What gear?"

"Well, it's an automatic, so you just put it in drive. But first, put your foot on the brake."

Gertrude's legs barely reached the pedals. "Can I slide the seat forward?"

"Oh for crying out loud. Yes, fine, go ahead."

"All right. How?"

"Reach down with your left hand. You'll feel a small button. Push it forward."

Gertrude tried to follow the directions, but she must have found the wrong button because the seat didn't go forward. It went up. "Wee!"

"Stop! That's the wrong button!"

"But I'm so tall!" she said.

"Stop!" Calvin repeated. "The forward button is right beside that one. Push it forward. I don't have all day."

"No? Why, what else do you have to do?"

"Hungry-Man and *Bonanza*. And the clock's ticking."

Her fingers found the right button, and she slid herself forward, and back down, till her feet could touch the pedals. She placed one foot on each.

"Move your left foot!" Calvin hollered.

"You don't have to holler, Calvin! I'm not deaf!"

"You only need your right foot. You'll move it back and forth between the brake, on the left, the most important part of the car in this case, and the gas pedal, on the right."

She put her foot on the brake and put the car in drive. "Now what?"

"Now," Calvin said, his face ashen, "you *very carefully* place your foot on the gas. Pretend there is an eggshell beneath—"

He didn't finish his sentence because his head snapped back against his headrest as the car lurched forward.

"Hi-ho, Silver!" Gertrude cried. "Away!"

The car picked up speed, but they were going in a straight line at least.

"That's enough, Gertrude! Slow down."

Gertrude did not slow down.

"Gertrude!" Calvin said, reaching for the handle suspended from the side of the windshield. "We are running out of parking lot!"

"I know!" Gertrude cackled and turned the car to the left.

"Gertrude! The school!"

"I see it, Calvin! It's a school! How can I not see a giant cement school?" She turned the car left again and picked up speed, sailing toward the football field. Then she turned left again.

Calvin swallowed hard, his knuckles white around the handle.

She turned left again, and then brought his precious Cadillac to an abrupt, whiplashing stop. "See?" she said with a victorious smile. "I can do it!"

"Get out," he snapped, and started to get out of the car.

"What? Why?" She had no idea why he was so upset. She thought she'd done a bang-up job.

"Get out, get out, get out," he said, as he came around the car toward her.

"But we haven't practiced going backward yet," she tried. He ignored her, so she put the car in reverse and stepped on the gas, leaving him standing alone with his shock as she sped away from him in reverse. She couldn't help it. She cackled. But her cackle was short-lived. She felt the car travel onto something that wasn't tar. She turned around to look and saw that she was on grass, and rapidly heading toward a chain-link fence. She slammed her foot onto the brake pedal and the car skidded to a stop. Relieved to see she had stopped with inches to spare, she turned her attention back to Calvin, who was actually running to the car. She couldn't believe it. She'd never seen him run before.

12

After the parking lot debacle, Gertrude steered clear of Calvin. But the calendar was creeping up on July 17, the date of the next poetry slam. She had to go, had to be there. She had no idea who had killed those kids and couldn't yet even prove they'd been killed by anyone other than bad luck. Plus, she had never gotten the chance to show John's picture to the cranky bartender.

She waited until Sunday morning to make her move. Then she looked around her trailer for something to bring Calvin as an I'm-sorry-for-almost-crashing-your-car gift. She thought about gifting him her newest cast-iron cat doorstop. She knew he'd really taken a shine to it, but then decided it was too heavy to carry all the way to his trailer. She thought about giving him a real, live kitten, but then decided that wouldn't be fair to the kitten. So she decided on a camouflage afghan. She couldn't remember where she'd gotten it, but she had never really liked the colors. She balled it up, shoved it under one arm, and headed out into the trailer park.

Of course, he didn't answer the door. She wiggled the doorknob. Locked. She was too short to see into any of the windows, but she knew he was in there. So she decided to knock again. And knock. And knock. She knew, without a doubt, that she could be more stubborn than he, so she just kept right on knocking. And after a mere two minutes and only slightly swollen knuckles, he ripped the door open.

"What?" he snapped.

"I brought you a present," she said, holding the afghan out.

He looked at it. Then at her. "I don't want that thing"

"I made it for you."

"No you didn't."

"Can I come in?"

"No." He started to shut the door.

"Calvin, wait!"

The door paused mid-swing. "I know why you're here," he said, "and the answer is no, I'm not driving you to Portland tomorrow." The door completed its swing.

Gertrude stood there in shock, staring at the closed door. *He is really, truly, actually mad this time.* She hollered through the door. "But you promised!"

Crickets.

"Calvin, I'm sorry! Just tell me what I can do to make it up to you!"

More crickets.

She set the afghan on his threshold and then, sadly, headed back up the street to her place. Then she called her friend G from church.

"You want me to do what? Drive you to Portland so you can go to a poetry reading? Gertrude, I love to help, but this job just sounds a little nuts."

"Please, G? It's a matter of life and death."

"Whose?"

"Well, I'm not sure. But someone has been killing poets."

"Why would anyone kill poets? Gertrude, I've got to go. We've got to get to church. If you really think someone's in danger, you need to call the police. I'm sorry, but I just can't take you to Portland."

"Well if you change your mind, give me a call, would ya?"

Someone knocked on Gertrude's door. She promptly hung up on G and hollered, "It's open!"

"Gertrude," Calvin said, stepping inside, "look at this." He was carrying a newspaper. He held it out to her, pointing to a small story beside a picture of Sexy Rose.

Gertrude drew a sharp breath. "She's dead?"

Calvin nodded, his lips pursed and colorless. "Maybe there really is something going on."

Gertrude wanted to say, "Of course there is!" but the situation being tender as it was, she let it go. She scanned the article. Her real name was Roseanne Waterford, but that was her face, no mistaking it. She had drowned in her own swimming pool. Swimming alone, in the middle of the night.

Alcohol was involved. Gertrude looked up at Calvin. "Is Alec really killing poets so he can win a poetry slam?"

"I don't know," Calvin muttered. "But maybe we should go tomorrow night. Ask some more questions."

Gertrude repressed a smile. She was thrilled Calvin had come around, but she was sorry Sexy Rose had had to die to make it happen. "All right then," she said.

"All right then." Calvin handed her the camouflage afghan. "Next time, I like donuts. Not scratchy yarn in July."

13

Gertrude thought she should wear the dog collar again. But the rest of the outfit, she changed up. Now that she'd seen how poets actually dressed, she realized that she could wear absolutely anything and fit right in. She went with a free cat food T-shirt she'd gotten by mailing in UPC codes and a pair of roomy bloomers. The bloomers were covered in large rose blossoms, and she thought the pants themselves were a pun. Hoped she might get some extra points for being so clever. The bloomers were homemade, but she hadn't made them. She couldn't remember where she'd gotten them, but right now, she was grateful for them, as she thought she looked absolutely dazzling.

Calvin didn't seem quite as impressed. "Those slacks look like curtains from a Japanese tea shop."

"They're not *slacks*, Calvin."

"No? What are they?"

"*Bloomers.*"

"Bloomers. All right. What happened to the purple lipstick?"

"Aw, shucks. I forgot. Can we stop at my trailer?"

"No."

She wanted to argue, but she thought she should wait until they were further from home before provoking him.

He pulled out onto Route 150 and headed south and out of Mattawooptock. "So what poem are you going to read tonight?"

"Why poem? Why not poems? Maybe I'll need more than one poem tonight."

"All right, so what *poems* are you going to read tonight?"

"You'll just have to wait and see."

Calvin barked out a derisive laugh. "You haven't written them yet, have you?"

"Of course I've written them. And they are brilliant. My new plan is to win this slam so that Alec will try to kill me."

"Oh, that's a great plan," Calvin said, his sarcasm thick.

"Thank you. I thought so."

They rode in a comfortable silence for a while. When they got to the toll booth, which cost one dollar, Gertrude handed Calvin forty cents.

"Gee, thanks."

"You're welcome. Can we stop at a drugstore?"

"No."

"Walmart?"

"No. You don't need lipstick, Gertrude."

"Calvin, you may have noticed, I'm competing with shiny, skinny young women all done up like circus whores."

Calvin laughed so hard, so suddenly, with such force, Gertrude wondered if he'd injured himself.

"What's so funny?"

"Horse!"

"What?"

"Horse!" he repeated, as he fought to get control of his emotions.

"What horse?"

Calvin took a deep, shaky breath. "The expression is circus *horse* not whores."

"Oh, well, that's what I said."

Calvin wiped at his eyes. "Oh, Gertrude. Thank you for making me laugh."

"You're welcome. Now can we stop at a drugstore?"

"Sure. We'll get off in Topsham. I could make a trip to the restroom anyway."

At Rite Aid, Gertrude doused herself with perfume samplers and then, wishing they had lipstick samples too, purchased a ninety-nine-cent blaze orange lipstick.

When she put it on in the car, Calvin said, "Well at least you won't get shot."

"Portland's not that dangerous, Calvin. Don't exaggerate."

"I meant by a hunter."

Gertrude looked away from the visor mirror and scowled. "It's not hunting season."

"Never mind."

Gertrude noticed the clock. Then she glanced at his speedometer. "Want me to drive? Then we could go the speed limit."

Calvin growled. "We don't need to be there until eight, remember? These people run on 'poet time,' whatever that means."

"Well, I want to get there early to talk to the bartender, and whoever else is there. So step on it."

They found a parking spot more expediently this time, and were able to park just down the street from Alfonso's Punk Rock Club. So, they were descending the shabby stairs at 7:45.

"Awful quiet," Calvin said.

Gertrude opened the door to find the bar still mostly deserted.

"Welcome back!" Chipper Jade chirped.

Gertrude ignored her and bent to the sign-up sheet.

Calvin, reaching for his wallet, asked, "If you don't want to start until eight, why don't you just say the event starts at eight?"

Jade took his money and said, "Because then people wouldn't show up until nine."

Gertrude headed toward the seats they'd occupied the week before.

"Gert, let's sit somewhere else, get a different vantage point."

Gertrude recoiled a bit at the suggestion of change, but then she realized he was right. "Maybe we should sit near the back," she said.

"Maybe we should," he said and headed toward the bar.

Gertrude followed. She climbed onto the barstool beside Calvin and then wondered what to do with her walker. Bar stools are not really conducive to walker storage, so she placed it immediately behind her, and it formed a protective hedge around her backside.

The bartender ignored them, but that didn't stop Calvin. "Could I get a glass of red wine, please?" Calvin hollered.

Without looking, Gertrude got her phone ready.

When the barkeep delivered Calvin's wine, Gertrude shoved her phone in his face. "Him!" she said.

The bartender recoiled. "What?"

"He's the one I was asking about. Do you know him? Have you seen him in here?"

He grudgingly took a closer look. "Not sure. Now, what'll you have?"

"What kind of an answer is that? Have you ever seen him before or not?"

"Still not sure. What can I get you?"

"Nothing for me."

"Stools are for drinkers."

"What?"

"Stools," the man spoke patronizingly slowly, "are ... for ... drinkers."

"She'll have a red wine," Calvin said.

The bartender turned around.

"I most certainly will not!" Gertrude cried, indignant.

"Calm down. I'll drink it. You just pretend to want it."

"Why does he want me to drink?"

"It's all about the cash, Gertrude. He's not going to make any money with you on that stool unless you drink."

"Well, you can't drink wine all night. You'll get all sauced and I'll have to drive home." She surprised herself with a giggle.

"I'll be fine. And you won't be driving anywhere."

"Well, hello, poet!" Ashes sang from behind them. "I was hoping you'd come back, Hazel!"

"Oh yeah, why's that?" Calvin asked before taking a dainty sip of wine.

"Because I know potential when I see it."

Gertrude usually had ample confidence in her abilities, but even she thought this comment was a bit suspect. "Did you hear about Rose?"

"No, what about her?"

Gertrude eyed Ashes closely, but it appeared she was telling the truth. "She died."

"What?" Ashes's eyes grew wide and filled with tears. "How?"

"She drowned."

Ashes appeared to be waiting for Gertrude to elaborate.

She did not.

"Drowned? Drowned where? As in, the ocean?"

"As in, her pool."

Ashes swore. "Well, that's just so sad. Was she drinking?"

"What makes you ask that?"

Ashes shrugged. "Rose drank a lot."

14

At a few minutes till eight, the bar started to fill up, and Gertrude started to make the rounds. She showed John's picture to at least twenty people, and at least twenty people claimed they'd never seen him before.

By the time Gertrude returned to her barstool, it was no longer available. "I thought you said you'd save my seat!"

"I said no such thing," Calvin replied.

"Well where am I supposed to sit?"

"I don't know. Why don't you go mingle?"

"I've been mingling! The show is going to start now. I need to settle in somewhere, so I can observe."

Calvin snorted. "Here. We'll take turns. Sit here for a few minutes, while I use the restroom." He slid off the stool.

Gertrude struggled to climb onto it.

"Can you do it?" Calvin asked, smirking.

"Yes. Why do these things have to be so dang high?"

"So that people who are standing at the bar are at the same level as those seated. And so the bartender doesn't get a bad back."

Gertrude looked up at him, one eyebrow cocked. "What, you some kind of barfly now?"

"I was a young man once," Calvin said thoughtfully, looking at himself in the mirror behind the bar.

Gertrude was uncomfortable. "Don't you have to go to the toilet?"

This startled him out of whatever nostalgic reverie he was having, and he was off. Gertrude wrapped her short fingers around the stem of his wine glass and looked around. She saw Bae approaching and braced herself for the hug.

"Hey, Hazel! Welcome back! Can I give you a big hug?"

Before Gertrude could come up with a declination, Bae had wrapped his arms around Gertrude from behind, squashing her walker up against her body with such force Gertrude almost spilled Calvin's wine.

"Well hello there, Bae. How are you?"

"I'm great! Fantastic!"

"That's nice. Do you know him?" Gertrude shoved her phone toward Bae.

Bae looked at it thoughtfully. "He does look familiar. But I can't place him. Sorry." He looked at Gertrude. "Is that the guy who, um, you know ..."

"Died? Yes. He's very dead."

Beth took the stage and welcomed everyone back to Poetland.

"I'm afraid I have some more bad news to impart. For those of you who haven't heard, Rose Waters died on Saturday night …"

Bae looked at Gertrude, wide-eyed. "What? First Abby, now Rose? What's going on?"

Gertrude was glad someone else was connecting the dots. "I know. It's pretty suspicious. You be careful. You're probably a target since you've qualified and all."

Bae looked incredulous. "Hazel, you can't possibly think … just because two poets are dead doesn't mean that they died because of poetry."

"Three," Gertrude said.

"Three?"

"Don't forget John."

"John was a poet too?"

"I don't know. But he was here."

Beth called up the first poet in the open mic.

Bae gave Gertrude a small smile, squeezed her arm and said, "Nobody kills anyone over poetry, Hazel." Bae disappeared into the crowd.

Calvin returned from the bathroom. "Scoot. My turn on the stool."

Gertrude didn't move. "Beth just announced Rose's death."

"I heard. Now scoot."

After a two-hour open mic, Beth announced the pre-slam break and directed all the slammers to the corner for the draw. Gertrude felt considerably more confident this time and was even having fun.

Ashes reached into the hat first, drew the one, and then said a naughty word.

Blaine the loud teacher reached in next, drew the seven, and then ate his paper.

All the other poets drew, and then it was Gertrude's turn. She reached into the hat and drew the last piece of crumpled paper. Unfolding it revealed an eight. She thought this was good, but she hesitated to celebrate, lest she was wrong.

After a brief history of slam, a quick recap of rules, and the calibration poet, Ashes took the stage. Gertrude was mesmerized once again. This girl might be a little fruity, but she sure had stage presence. Gertrude scanned the crowd, looking for anyone who looked as if they might want to murder Ashes. It was hard to do from the back, so Gertrude left Calvin and pushed her way to the front of the room, earning dozens of dirty looks on her way.

An old upright piano stood adjacent to the stage like an ancient sentinel. A young man sat on the piano bench. Gertrude plopped down beside him. The bench creaked beneath them. Beer sloshed onto the young man's knee.

She scanned the room again, not finding anyone who looked murderous, but she was happy to see that two of the judges appeared to be even older than she was. *Well that shouldn't hurt my scores any.*

All five judges liked Ashes's poem and gave her a 26. Gertrude watched Ashes's face as the score was announced, but it was stoical.

Next up was Bubbles. Again, Gertrude scanned the crowd, but they all appeared to be innocent avid poetry-listeners. Bubbles went over three minutes, earning a time penalty and a score of 24.

After some supportive applause, Alec took the stage. Gertrude squinted, concentrating. There was just something off about this guy. His mohawk was bright and high tonight and stood out even more against his pizza delivery uniform. He performed a poem about cleaning pools. The crowd thought it was hilarious. Gertrude didn't get it. Judges gave him a 27. Ashes looked furious.

It was Thor's turn. Thor hollered out a poem about Spanx. Gertrude didn't get this one either. She had no idea what Spanx were, but she noticed the mature female judges gave him a pair of sixes. This made her happy. Thor finished with a 25.1.

Beth called out Sinclair's name, and he started to sing before he even stood up. His rich baritone voice rang loud and true as he gracefully sauntered to the stage. Gertrude hadn't even known that singing was allowed. *I'll have to try that*, she thought. *Next week. Unless I catch the killer tonight. Then we probably won't come next week.* This thought made her sad, but not sad enough to delay the killer-catching. Sinclair sang the beginning and ending of his poem, stopping in the middle to bemoan the loss of payphones. Gertrude didn't understand. Apparently, neither did the judges, giving him a 25.2. He looked devastated. Ashes was smiling.

Zest jogged to the stage. Gertrude was glad. She liked Zest. Thought she was ... zesty. The judges gave Zest's poem about Aretha Franklin a 22. The room erupted into boos.

Blaine, in all his tattooed glory, stepped into the spotlight. Then he began to shout statistics about school shootings. The audience began to snap. As Blaine continued, he picked up volume and intensity. Sweat poured down his temples. He grabbed the microphone with one hand and hollered so loud his voice cracked. Then he picked up the mic stand with his other hand, still hollering. Then, much to Gertrude's fright, he took three quick steps and leapt onto the top of the piano. She looked up at him and his sweat dripped down on her. He was still screaming. Still holding the mic stand. She wondered where that burly bouncer from last week was. Surely this was a bootable offense.

Blaine finished his poem, and then threw the mic stand and the microphone onto the stage, creating a terrific boom. Gertrude suddenly wished she hadn't left Calvin. She missed his commentary at the moment. Blaine jumped off the piano and returned to his seat along the wall opposite hers. She realized her mouth was hanging open and she snapped it shut.

Beth righted the microphone stand, straightened the mic, and then gently reminded everyone that we only have one mic stand, and if we break it, we won't have another one.

The judges gave him a 29.

Gertrude felt positively demure following that spectacle. She didn't even hesitate this time. Her feet confidently carried her to and up onto the stage and she turned to face the crowd with a flourish. As the crowd quieted, Gertrude took a deep breath and smiled. This time, she had her poem memorized.

15

Sometimes we feel guilty.
  Sometimes we do things
heavier than us, things
that stick to our backs.
We break hearts.
We spill secrets. We forget to say
I love you. Or worse.
Once I did something so heavy
I thought it would kill me.
For days, weeks, I dragged
my feet around waiting to be
found out or to crumble
beneath the weight, whichever
came first. But I was wrong.
Confession came first.
Confession stood between
crumbling and me, stood
between me and my end.

And it was a friend.
She heard my words, she
took them in, and held them
without judging. She set
me free of the weight.
I couldn't thank her, didn't
get the chance, but I can
show her my gratitude
by taking your weight from you.
If you have done something,
something that has left you
heavy, you can tell me.
Let me take your weight from
you. Bear it for you. Set you free.
All you have to do is tell me.

Gertrude stopped. No one clapped. So she said, "The end." Then the room erupted in applause. Feeling heady with pride, she climbed off the stage and, after an amicable nod to the young man on the piano bench, made her way to the bar and Calvin.

One side of his mouth was smiling.

"Can I get a glass of water?" she asked the bartender.

He rolled his eyes, and it wasn't clear whether he was going to oblige.

"Pretty clever, aren't you?" Calvin said.

"Yes. I am clever."

"You're making a pretty big assumption, though, Gert."

The bartender handed her a grimy glass of water. She took a sip. "What's that?"

"You're assuming our killer feels remorse."

The judges held the scorecards up in the air, and Beth began to read them aloud, "6.2 ..." The crowd booed. "7.3, a 9, another 9, and our evening's first 10!" The crowd went wild.

Gertrude didn't want to admit it, but she was shocked. She made sure, however, to hide that shock from Calvin.

Beth announced Gertrude's score, "Drop the high, drop the low, and that gives Hazel a 25.3!"

"Whoa!" Calvin exclaimed.

"Why so shocked, Calvin?"

Calvin looked down at the bar and Gertrude noticed that he'd been keeping score on a napkin. "Well, I can't believe I'm saying this, but you just advanced to the second round." He looked at her. He lowered his voice, "Do you have another poem?"

"Of course I have another poem!"

"That concludes round one of our qualifying slam! Don't forget to support our venue by buying drinks, and don't forget to tip your bartender! Now, it's time for round two! Let's welcome Blaine back to the stage!"

"Yes, let's," Calvin said. "Let's also call the fire department."

Gertrude looked at him.

"So they can dig us out when he causes the building to collapse on us."

Calvin gave Gertrude a turn on the barstool. Blaine read a calm, gentle love poem. The judges ate it up, giving him a 27. Next up, Ashes recited a hypnotic poem about harnessing the power of the moon. She got a 28. Alec took the stage for a rousing retelling of Beowulf. Got a 23.

Calvin leaned toward Gertrude, "You need a 30.7 to make it to the final round."

"All right," Gertrude said, distractedly.

"No, it's not all right. That's an impossible score."

Gertrude glared at him. "Then why did you tell me that?"

Calvin shrugged. "Just trying to help."

Beth welcomed Hazel back to the stage.

Gertrude had lied to Calvin. She didn't have another poem. So she decided to make one up. "I have a cat named Hail," she announced. "He has a fuzzy tail." Some snickers in the front row. This gave her an idea. "He loves to eat Snickers bars." Some genuine laughter this time. She thought she should rhyme. *What rhymes with Snickers bars?* "He likes chick memoirs." More laughter. They were really laughing at her. In a good way. She couldn't believe it. "He's the best cat in town. He never lets me down." The laughter had stopped, but they still looked at her expectantly, smiling, as if just waiting for the next punchline. Trouble was, she didn't have one. She was stuck. She decided to shift gears. "I also know a cop named Hale." Silence. Expectant stares. "He does not have a nice tail." The place erupted. While the laughter was shocking, it was also contagious. Gertrude giggled. *Golly, this is fun.* "I don't know if he likes Snickers. But he does like his liquor." She wasn't sure if this was true, but it almost rhymed. "He might be the best cop in town, but he's still a real clown. The end." Gertrude stepped off the stage.

Beth tried to calm the crowd down, but it took a while.

Gertrude made her way to the back but was accosted before reaching Calvin. She didn't hear her scores because suddenly there was a very drunk man in her face.

"I have something I'd like to confess," the man said, spitting in Gertrude's face.

"All right, what?"

"I cheated on my wife."

Gertrude let go of her walker and pushed him in the chest with both hands. The man, looking shocked, fell backward into his chair. Gertrude walked past him toward Calvin.

"What was that all about?" Calvin asked.

"It was a poem about my cat and Deputy Hale."

"No, not that. The man you just assaulted."

"Oh, that? He cheated on his wife."

Calvin laughed. "And he just confessed that to you?" He laughed again. "Wow, I guess that's the power of poetry. It was good of you to be so gracious with him."

"Gracious? I don't have time to be gracious!"

16

The final round came down to Ashes and Blaine. Order was decided by a coin toss. Blaine won and decided to let Ashes go first. She delivered a tear-jerking poem about her little brother's struggle with cancer.

The bartender groaned.

Gertrude turned around to give him a dirty look.

"Kid doesn't even have a brother," he said.

Judges didn't care, however, and gave her a 29.

Blaine took the stage.

"Calvin, he doesn't look so good."

"Just a little tipsy is all."

Blaine started his poem, sounding relatively like himself, but then he just stopped. The crowd, assuming he had just forgotten a line, started snapping encouragingly.

"Something's wrong," Gertrude said.

Blaine lost his balance, staggered to the side a foot, then righted himself. He let go of the microphone, grinned at the audience apologetically, and then collapsed right on his rump. It was like watching the world's hairiest toddler fall down.

"Did I say fire department?" Calvin asked. "I meant ambulance."

Blaine giggled and then got up on his hands and knees, flashed another smile at the poetry fans, and then pulled himself to his feet. "Sorry about that, folks. I think I'm done."

To Gertrude's surprise, Beth still asked the judges to score his faux pas, and they did, gently.

Ashes won. She had finally qualified.

"There. Now maybe the killing will stop," Calvin said.

"You can't think Ashes is the killer? She doesn't need to kill. She's too good! She can win without killing people."

"If you say so. Let's go." He stood up and threw a few bucks on the bar.

"Actually, I want to go check on Blaine."

"Fine. Hurry up." Calvin sat back down.

"Want to come with me?"

"Not really."

Gertrude bulldozed her way through the crowd until she reached a sleepy Blaine. "You all right there, young fella?"

He looked up and smiled at her. "Sure," he said slowly.

"Do you have a way to get home?"

"Sure," he said in the same manner.

Gertrude waited for him to elaborate.

He did not.

"Blaine?" She waved a hand in his face. "You in there?"

"Sure."

"How are you getting home?"

Blaine looked confused.

"Would you like a ride?"

"Sure."

"All right, ya big lug." She grabbed his right arm and tried to heft it onto her shoulders. It flopped back down to his side.

"Sorry," he slurred.

"Come on. You're going to have to help me." She wrapped her arm around his waist and said, "Up, up, up," as she pulled. He came out of his chair with her grunt and his moan. He wobbled on his feet, and then put his right hand on her walker to steady himself. "Good, just like that." Together, they took one shaky step. Then another.

"What are you trying to do?" Ned asked, grabbing Blaine on his other side.

Gertrude panted. "Got to"—breath, breath—"get him"—breath, breath—"to the car"—breath, breath— "right outside."

"OK, here we go," Ned said.

Gertrude caught Calvin's eye and jerked her head toward the door.

He didn't look happy.

Gertrude stopped helping when they got to the stairs. She had just run right out of gumption.

Ned helped Blaine up the stairs, one painful step at a time, and then out into the night.

"Our car is that way," Gertrude said pointing.

"Good," Ned puffed. "Downhill."

"*Our* car?" Calvin repeated.

"Shh," Gertrude said.

"Which one?" Ned asked.

Gertrude pointed. "The Cadillac." Then her arm dropped to her side. "Uh-oh."

Ned and Blaine stopped. "This one?" Ned asked.

Gertrude nodded.

Calvin caught up to them then and made a sort of choking sound.

The streetlight illuminated Calvin's car, giving them all a great view of the words "your next" keyed nearly the length of the car.

"Twasn't me," Blaine said.

"No kidding," Ned said. "Probably wasn't a poet at all, since they spelled 'you're' wrong."

"Unless they want us to think they're not a poet," Gertrude said.

"What?" Ned said. Then, "Can we put him in the car? He's kind of heavy."

"Calvin, unlock the car," Gertrude said.

Calvin made no move to oblige. He just stood there in the streetlight, staring at his car.

"Are you crying?" Gertrude asked.

Calvin didn't answer.

"Calvin!" Gertrude hollered. "Open the door! Ned has helped us, but he's not going to stand here all night!"

Calvin snapped out of it, looked at Ned, and then looked at Gertrude. "Helped *us*? He's not helping me! I don't want this drunken fool in my car!"

"Hey!" Blaine cried.

"He didn't mean it, Blaine," Gertrude said.

"No, look!" Blaine said, pointing.

A blur of motion had darted out from the shadows behind them and was now running down the street. Gertrude took off. She stayed on the sidewalk as long as she could, but then she saw him dart down a side street. She started to cross the street, causing a cab to come to a screeching stop and the cab driver to swear at her. "Sorry!" she called over her shoulder! "And your mother should really wash that mouth out with some soap!" Once safely across the street, she stopped. She'd lost him. "Oh, horsefeathers!" she said. Then she saw the hoodied crook slinking along a dark wall. "Hey! You! Stop!" She tore after him, but soon lost sight of him again. She came to an intersection and looked around wildly. Then she saw him. Under a porch light, struggling to unlock the door. "Hey!" she cried. He looked at her and she recognized his face. "Alec?"

"Quiet!" he said. "Go away!"

"No I won't go away!" she said, shambling toward him. She climbed the steps as he continued to struggle with his keys. "Is this your house?" she asked.

"None of your business." He looked around in a panic.

"What are you so afraid of?" Gertrude looked around too, but there was no one in sight. Only brick houses, cars, and shadows. "Are you afraid of the shadows?"

He finally got the key to turn and pushed his way inside.

Gertrude pushed right in after him.

"Hey!" he cried. "What are you doing?"

Just then, Calvin pulled up in front of the house. Blaine was leaning against the passenger side window, sound asleep, drooling on the glass. Calvin jumped out of the Cadillac. "Gertrude!" he shouted. "Are you all right?"

"Gertrude?" Alec repeated, looking at Gertrude.

Calvin hurried up the steps, breathing hard.

"What is this?" Alec asked. "Who are you people?"

Calvin stepped inside. "Gertrude, give me your cellular telephone."

"Why?" Gertrude cried.

"So I can call the police."

"Why?" Alec and Gertrude cried in unison.

"Because this little punk vandalized my car, that's why!"

"I didn't vandalize anything!"

Calvin stepped toward him. "You sniveling little liar!"

"Don't call me a liar!"

"Wait!" Gertrude shouted. She stepped between them and placed one hand on each of their chests. "Just wait a minute!" She looked at Alec. "Do you have a cat?"

"What?" Alec and Calvin asked in unison.

Gertrude looked at Calvin. "If we're going to interrogate him, we should let him hold a cat." She looked at Alec. "Now, do you have a cat, or do I have to go find one?"

17

The three of them sat in Alec's living room. Gertrude and Calvin sat side by side on a loveseat. Alec sat in a glider, holding his cat.

"Alec, are you saying that you did not key Calvin's car?"

"I did not."

"Gertrude, why are you listening to him? Of course he's the one. Why else would he be lurking in the shadows?"

"I was lurking in the shadows because I owe someone some money. I saw him on the street just before you guys came out, so I was just going to wait until he'd passed. Then I heard a noise behind me in the alley. I thought it was him, so I took off."

"Why do you owe him some money?" Gertrude asked.

"None of your business."

"Why do you owe him some money?" Gertrude repeated.

Alec sighed and rolled his eyes. "He sold me something, all right? And I told him I'd pay him later. But I haven't yet."

"Did you kill Abby Livingstone?"

Alec's eyes grew big, and his hand paused atop the cat's head. The cat wiggled to get the hand going again. "What? Of course not. Didn't Abby die in a car accident?"

"She did. Did you kill Rose Waters?"

Alec shook his head. "Who are you people? I think you should go. I didn't touch your car." He started to get up, spilling the cat in the process.

"Sit down," Calvin ordered.

Alec sat back down.

"Pick the cat back up," Gertrude ordered.

Alec complied. "Look, I'm a little messed up right now, so maybe I'm imagining all this. But just in case I'm not, you guys know you're pretty weird, right?"

"Did you see who did key my car?"

"No man. I don't care about your stupid car." Alec swore.

"Watch your mouth," Gertrude said. "Calvin and I are experienced gumshoes. We have been hired to catch Abby's killer. She was murdered. So was Rose. So was John Crane. I think you're our guy."

"Who's John Crane?"

Gertrude took out her phone, stabbed at the screen, then held the picture out to Alec.

He squinted. "I don't even know that guy."

"Well he was at the slam the night Abby won—"

"Oh! Wait! Let me look again."

She held the phone out.

He took it and started scrolling.

"What are you doing?"

"Looking at other pics of the guy. I think that he might have been a judge that night. Yeah, I'm pretty sure he was. I remember him because he kept giving me crap scores." He swore again.

"He was a judge?"

Alec nodded. "I think so." He handed the phone back to her.

She looked at Calvin. "So, Abby wins a slam. The next night, she dies. The next night, the judge dies." She looked at Alec. "If someone judges a slam, can they come back and judge again, another slam?"

"I've never seen that happen."

"All right then." Gertrude chewed that over. "It makes sense why you'd kill Abby and Rose. But it doesn't make sense why you'd kill the judge, unless it was for revenge, and if it was for revenge, it doesn't make sense why you'd wait two days."

Alec leaned forward. "Lady, it doesn't make sense why anyone would kill any of these people. Do you realize that the person who goes to nationals has to *pay* to go to nationals? They have to pay for their travel, pay for the hotel, pay to compete. And if they win? You know what they get if they win? One person out of seventy gets *some* money. It's an undisclosed amount. And you know why it's undisclosed? Because it's not much. It's probably just enough to pay for their plane ticket. I am telling you, these people were not killed because of poetry. No one dies because of poetry."

"Tell that to Pablo Neruda," Calvin muttered.

"Who?" Alec and Gertrude asked.

"Never mind," Calvin said.

"Alec, if no one is killing over poetry, then why did someone key a threat into our car?" Gertrude asked.

"Maybe it was the tow truck driver." Alec smirked.

"You're not funny," Gertrude said.

"Gert, I don't think this kid knows anything. And I still think we should call the police, let them fingerprint the car and—"

"No!" Alec cried. "No police."

"Why?" Gertrude asked. "If you're so innocent, why the fuss?"

"Because I'm on parole. And because if my dealer sees the cops roll up to my door, I am in serious trouble."

"Your dealer?" Calvin said. "Didn't you just get out of rehab?"

Alec tilted his head to the side, looking amused. "That was just a poem, man."

"I don't think he did it," Gertrude said. "I don't like him. I think he's definitely a criminal. But I don't think he's our killer."

"Gee, thanks," Alec said.

"Come on, Calvin." Gertrude patted his knee and stood up. "Let's go."

"That's it?" Calvin asked.

"What else do you want to do to him?"

"I think he keyed my car." He looked at Alec. "Spell 'you're next.'"

"What?"

"Spell 'you're next,'" he repeated slowly.

He spelled it. Correctly.

"As I said before," Gertrude said. "The poet probably spelled it wrong on purpose." She looked at Alec. "You going to blow my cover?"

"You mean your cover as Hazel the terrible poet? Nah, I won't blow that."

"You're a nasty creature, you know that?" Gertrude said.

"He is, and I'm done talking. The kid keyed my car. I'm calling the cops. Give me your phone."

"Ashes!" Alec cried.

Gertrude and Calvin turned to look at him.

"What about her?" Gertrude said.

"Ashes keyed your car. I saw her."

18

When they got back to the car, Blaine was still asleep. Calvin had to shake him forcefully to jolt him into consciousness.

"What?" Blaine looked around in confusion.

"What's your address?" Calvin asked.

Blaine blinked, wiped his mouth, and looked out the windows. "Where am I?"

"Never mind that. What's your address?"

"Twenty-two Ocean View, apartment B."

"You can afford an ocean view on a teacher's salary?"

"There isn't really an ocean view. It's just a street name. And I live there with four other people."

"Gertrude, can you plug that address into your GPS?"

"No need to," Blaine said, sounding more sober now. "If you just get me back to Congress, I can give you directions."

Calvin put the car in drive.

"Blaine?" Gertrude said from the backseat.

"Yeah?"

"How much did you have to drink tonight?"

He scratched his head. "I don't really remember. Wow, guess I made quite a fool of myself, huh?"

"Well, do you normally act like that? I mean, when you drink?" she asked. "Or was tonight different?"

"I dunno. I was acting pretty normal till the end. But no, I've never forgotten my poem and fallen down on stage before."

"So you normally jump on pianos?" Calvin asked.

"Oh yeah. All the time. If there's a piano, I jump on it. It's sort of my shtick."

"Well, it's asinine. You're a teacher. You should hold yourself to higher standards," Calvin said.

"My students adore me. They love poetry and they love poetry slam. And they are leading the state in language arts standardized test scores." Blaine looked at Calvin. "Maybe things have changed a bit since you were in school." He looked out the windshield. "Take a right here."

Gertrude could almost feel the rage emanating from Calvin. "So, Blaine, sounds like you got a little drunker than you meant to. Do you suppose someone could have slipped something into your drink?"

"To what end? I don't think so. I think I just had too much to drink on an empty stomach. This is it right here on the right."

Calvin slowed and pulled alongside the curb.

Blaine started to get out. Then he looked at Calvin. "Thanks a lot for the ride, guys. Sorry to have been so much trouble. I owe you one."

Calvin didn't say anything, so Gertrude said, "You betcha!"

Blaine got out of the car. Gertrude did too so that she could slide into the front. She watched Blaine walk inside as Calvin drove away.

"I just don't believe it," Gertrude said.

"Which part?"

"She's so talented. So smart. So pretty. Why would she be running around drugging people and keying cars?"

Calvin pulled onto Congress Street. "I don't know, Gert. But you're making a lot of guesses and counting them as facts. We don't know that she drugged anyone. And we don't even know if she keyed my car. I'm not so sure we should have believed that rug rat, Alec. I'm still thinking we should have called the—"

"Oh Mylanta!" Gertrude cried.

"What?"

"Look!" She pointed over her right shoulder. "Turn around!"

"What? Why?"

"I just saw Dave!"

"Dave? The northern Maine poison-your-water-spook Dave?"

"Yeah! That one! Turn around!"

"I'm not turning around, Gertrude. I want to go home."

"Please?"

"No."

"Pretty please with pickles on top?"

"No."

Gertrude thought she was going to cry. She really wanted to see Dave again. She couldn't stand not knowing who he really was, or what he had been doing hiding out in the Maine forest with a cabin full of guns.

"It probably wasn't even him, Gertrude. We're in the city. So many people. You're bound to see someone who looks like—"

"It was Dave. I ought to remember the man who tried to kill me."

"He didn't try to kill you, Gertrude. He saved your life. You and all those other women."

"I saved them first," she mumbled. Then she crossed her arms and closed her eyes, leaning back on the headrest.

A few minutes later, she felt Calvin pull onto the interstate. "Can I drive?" she asked without opening her eyes.

"No."

"I thought not, but I figured I'd ask," she said and fell sound asleep.

It was 3:54 a.m. when Calvin pulled into the trailer park. He shook Gertrude awake. "We're home."

Gertrude yawned and stretched. "All right," she said.

He stopped in front of her trailer. "Gertrude, I'm really tired. Let me sleep in tomorrow, or today, actually, OK?"

"All right."

"No, I mean it. I need a few days to recover. I'm way too old to be staying up till dawn."

"It's not dawn yet."

"You know what I mean. Now get out of my car."

19

A t ten the next morning, Gertrude called Ashes. She answered on the first ring. "Hi, Ashes. This is Hazel Walker, from the poetry slam? I was wondering if you would give me some coaching next week before the slam? Now that you've qualified, I was thinking you could help me qualify. I would like to win next week. I don't have any money to pay you, but you said maybe we could do a few free lessons?"

"Sure, Hazel! Absolutely! Why don't you meet me at the gazebo on the Eastern Prom? How about six?"

Gertrude had no idea what she'd just said, but she wrote it down anyway. "Eastern Prom," she muttered as she wrote. "All right. Got it. Hey, Ashes? Do you have time right now for a few questions?"

"Sure."

"Great. You said you knew John Crane, right?"

"No?"

"Yes, you did. You said you knew him, had talked to him a few times."

"So, what's your question exactly?"

"My question is, *where* did you talk to him a few times?"

"Oh, I don't remember, just around. Bars and stuff."

"Which bars?"

"Hazel, I really don't remember. Why does this matter?"

"It probably doesn't. All right, Ashes. Thank you for your help. I'll see you Monday." Gertrude hung up and hurried down the street to tell Calvin her new plan.

She pounded on Calvin's door.

"Gertrude!" he hollered through the door. "I told you to leave me alone! I'm sleeping!"

"You're not sleeping! I can hear the television!" she hollered back. "Sounds like *Gunsmoke!*"

"I can sleep with the TV on. Now go away!"

She pounded again. "Calvin, open up! I need you! I've got a plan! You've got to take me to Portland!"

There were a few seconds of silence, and Gertrude thought she'd made some headway, but then Calvin said, "Not today, Gert. I'm serious. When I get up, I've got to go get the car fixed. Now leave me alone, or I won't take you on Monday either!"

Yikes! That would be problematic. She stepped back, unsure of how to proceed. Then she had an idea. She took her time getting back to her trailer. Then she sat down on the front steps. A cat curled around each leg. "Hi, Nor'easter. Good to see you outside, sweetie. Hi, Blizzard, you're looking awfully lean today. Remind me later and I'll give you some extra kibble. Got to plump you up a bit." She called the CAP bus.

"Community Action Program Transportation," a robotic-sounding voice answered. "What is your location?"

"Can you tell me if Andrea is on duty today?"

Nothing but fuzz.

"Hello?" Gertrude said.

"We are not supposed to give out personal information about our volunteers. Do you need transportation?"

"Tell you what. I'm at 3 Birchwood Drive. If Andrea's on duty, send a van. If she's not, don't bother." Gertrude hung up.

Andrea pulled into the park ten minutes later.

Gertrude gave her a big smile and a small wave. Then she heaved herself to a standing position and headed toward the van on cramping legs.

She slid the door open and climbed in.

"I heard you asked for me by name?" Andrea said, sounding amused.

"Yep." She slammed the door shut. "I need you to take me to Portland."

"Gertrude, I can't take you to Portland! I—"

Gertrude waved a hand in the air. "I know, necessary stops, ya, ya, ya, but never mind all that. I need to get to Portland. And I need you to take me. It's a matter of life and death."

Andrea paused. Then, "Gertrude, I just can't. If I tell them, they'll fire me. If I just sneak off, they'll find me and fire me."

"Isn't this a volunteer position?"

"Still doesn't mean I want to get into trouble!"

Gertrude rolled her eyes. "Fine. Don't you have your own car?"

"Yeah," Andrea said hesitantly.

"Great. Then we'll take your car."

Andrea didn't say anything.

"Andrea, I gave you a cat."

"And I'm grateful for that, Gertrude, but I'm in the middle of a shift here. And well—"

"Well, you don't want to drive me to Portland, and I don't really care. Do you want me to tell Deputy Hale of the Somerset County Sheriff's Department what you've been up to with the homeless people's food stamp cards?"

Andrea looked indignant. "Are you blackmailing me?"

"No, Andrea. I am simply asking you to take me to Portland."

Andrea looked as if she might cry. But she put the van in drive.

Andrea drove to the Community Action Program office. She parked in front. "My Subaru's out back. The green one. It's unlocked if you want to get in. I'll be right there." They both climbed out, Andrea to go talk to her supervisor, and Gertrude to find the Subaru.

It wasn't hard. It was the only car in the lot. Gertrude leaned against it and waited.

Andrea reappeared within minutes. "You can get in!"

"Can I put my walker in the backseat?"

"Of course."

Gertrude did, though it was a tighter fit than Calvin's Cadillac. Gertrude shut the door and then slid into the front. "Ow!" she cried.

"What?"

"Burnt my fanny on these fancy leather seats!"

"Oh." Andrea started the car and rolled down the windows. "So where are we going in Portland?"

"SMCC."

"The college?"

"Yep."

"And why are we going there?"

"To catch a murderer."

Andrea stopped the car. "Gertrude, is this going to be dangerous?"

"Don't you worry a bit. We won't be in any danger. We just need to ask a few questions. You can even stay in the car if you want. Or if you want to be my assistant, I promise to protect you."

20

Gertrude snored all the way to South Portland. When Andrea pulled onto the SMCC campus, she shook Gertrude.

"I'm awake! I'm awake!" She looked around, squinting.

"Now where do we go?"

"Now we find the dorm."

"The dorm's open in July?"

"Yep." She had no idea.

"There's only one dorm?"

"Not sure. We'll find out. Here, pull right up to that young man right there."

Andrea pulled the car ahead a few hundred feet.

Gertrude rolled down the window and stuck her head out. "Excuse me, young fella. I'm looking for the roommate of John Crane. Do you know where I could find him?"

The student laughed, but then just looked confused. "I don't know, ma'am."

"Don't call me ma'am. Can you tell me his name?"

"John's roommate's name?"

"Yes."

He shoved his hands in his pockets. "I don't know."

"It's all right," Gertrude reassured him. "You can tell me. I'm a gumshoe."

He hesitated. Then, "His name is Scottie. He lives in the dorm." He pointed. "Second floor. But I'm not sure what room."

"All right. Thank you." She looked at Andrea. "Drive."

Andrea drove.

"Just pull right up to that side door there," Gertrude said.

"I don't think I can park there."

"Well just drop me off and go park in the parking lot."

Andrea looked disappointed.

"What?"

"I just ... I kind of wanted to go in with you. You know, see you in action."

This pleased Gertrude immensely. "All right. Drop me off by the door. You go park. And I'll wait for you."

Andrea did as she was told, and left Gertrude by the side of the dorm in the sun. But only for a few minutes. She soon reappeared, a little out of breath. Gertrude waited for her to open the door, which she did, and Gertrude walked in ahead of her. Then she looked up the stairs and groaned.

"It's OK, we'll go slow," Andrea said.

"I don't need to go slow. I just don't like stairs." Gertrude went up the stairs as fast as she could, just to prove a point.

So she reached the second floor completely winded and again waited for Andrea to open the door. She pushed past her without a thank you and, before Andrea could catch her, knocked on the first door she came to.

A girl with long blonde hair opened it.

"Hello," Gertrude said. "I'm looking for Scottie. Do you know what room he lives in?"

The girl looked unsure of how to respond. Finally, she said, "Scottie who?"

Gertrude looked her up and down. "I'm not sure how Scottie would feel about me telling you his last name."

Andrea stepped toward the open door. "I'm sorry. This is Scottie's grandmother."

Gertrude glared at her.

Andrea continued, "She wants to see her grandson. But she's forgotten his room number."

"Oh," the girl said sweetly. "What's her grandson's last name?"

Andrea looked at Gertrude, who shrugged. "I don't think she remembers. But he was John Crane's roommate, if that helps."

The girl gasped. "Oh! Of course. Yes, well, John lived in 202."

"OK, great. Thanks." Andrea started to walk away.

Gertrude stayed planted, staring at the girl.

"Was there something else?" the girl asked.

"You knew John Crane?"

"A little."

"You know how he died?"

The girl nodded.

"Do you really think he drank himself to death?"

"Gertrude!" Andrea scolded.

The girl shrugged. "That's what they're saying. Why?"

"Well, was he that type of young man? Was he ... a sot?"

"A sot?" The girl looked baffled.

"A sot ... a ... was he a regular boozer?"

The girl shrugged again. "No more than the rest of us, I guess." She stepped back as if she wanted to be done with the conversation.

"Come on, Gertrude," Andrea said, pulling on her arm.

"Don't yank me around. I'm coming, I'm coming," Gertrude said. "I don't think the kid drank himself to death. I think he was murdered."

The door to Room 202 stood ajar. Gertrude whacked it with her walker anyway. "Hello? Anybody home?"

A young man materialized in the doorway. "Yes?"

"May we come in?" Gertrude asked and started to push her way inside.

Andrea grabbed her arm, not quite successfully holding her back, but at least stalling her progress.

"I'm not really in the habit of letting strange women into my dorm room." He stepped out into the hallway and shut the door. "What can I do for you?"

"Well that's a good deal suspicious," Gertrude said, eyeing the door as if trying to see through it.

The young man looked at Andrea and raised an eyebrow.

"Gertrude," she said.

"What?"

"Ask your questions. He's waiting."

"Andrea," she said, exasperated, "I have a system here. You said you wouldn't interfere."

"I said no such thing."

Gertrude looked at the young man. "Are you Scottie?"

He nodded. "Guilty."

"You might not want to be throwing that word around," Gertrude said.

"Why's that?"

"Because I think someone murdered John Crane."

Scottie stared at Gertrude for a few seconds, seeming to absorb her words. Then he reached behind and turned the doorknob. "Come on in."

The women entered the room, Andrea gingerly and Gertrude confidently. The latter plopped down on a futon and let out a deep breath. "Feels good to take a load off."

He sat down in a desk chair. "So, who are you again?"

"I am a gumshoe, and I am investigating John Crane's death—"

"Why?"

"Why?" Gertrude repeated, incredulous.

"Yes, why? They're saying it was an accident, so what makes you think it wasn't? And why are you investigating? Did someone hire you?"

"I'll be asking the questions, thank you."

Scottie leaned back in his chair. He held one hand out to her briefly, inviting her to proceed.

"Tell me what happened that night."

"The night John died?"

Gertrude nodded.

Scottie sighed. "Sure. Well, it was just like any other night, at first. It was a Wednesday, and I'll tell you, John *never* drank on Wednesdays. He wasn't much of a drinker anyway. But definitely not on Wednesdays. He had an eight o'clock class the next morning. So, John didn't come home after dinner. When it got late, I texted him. He said he was with a girl and to leave him alone."

"A girl? What girl?"

Scottie shrugged. "Wish I knew. Someone hot enough to get him to drink on a Wednesday."

"Where did they find him again?" Gertrude asked, even though she had no idea.

"In his car. Alone."

Gertrude rubbed her chin, thinking. Then, "Did you know Abby Livingstone?"

"Sure. John dated her for a while."

"Bingo!" Gertrude cried.

"What?" Scottie asked.

"Nothing. So, how long did they date?"

"A few months. Nothing serious, I don't think. I mean, I know it wasn't serious on John's part. And she broke up with him, so I guess it wasn't serious on her part either."

"Why'd they break up?"

"No idea."

"You didn't ask?"

"I didn't care." His expression grew sadder.

"Do you know what room Abby lived in?"

"Why?"

"I'd like to talk to her roommate."

"She had a single. One of the reasons John liked her so much."

Gertrude didn't get the connection. "Do you know Ashes LaFlamme?"

Scottie shook his head. "Don't think so."

"Hang on." Gertrude reached into her walker pouch. As she groped around for her phone, she asked, "Did the cops ever talk to you?"

"About John's death?"

"A-yuh." She pulled the phone out and opened Facebook.

"Nope."

She found Ashes's profile pic and held it out toward Scottie. "Ever seen her before?"

"Nope. Wish I had."

"So, the night before Abby died, John went to a poetry reading. Did you know about that?"

Scottie snorted. "Sure did. He said some hottie had asked him to go be a judge at a poetry slam."

Gertrude's eyes grew wide. "Someone other than Abby asked him?"

"Well, yeah, because if Abby had asked him, he would have just said that. But he didn't say any name. He just said she was hot."

"When you do not find a female attractive, do you say that she is cold?" Gertrude asked.

"What?"

"Never mind. Did he say anything when he got back from the poetry reading?"

"He did." Scottie looked guilty. "I didn't really pay much attention. Wish I had." He closed his eyes and scrunched up his face. Gertrude thought he looked like a toddler trying to poop. "I think he said that he'd messed up the plan. That he was supposed to help the hot girl win, but then he wanted to make Abby happy, so he helped her win—"

"What?" Gertrude interrupted. "Judges aren't supposed to *help* anyone win. They're not even supposed to know any of the poets. That's something they ask right up front."

Scottie shrugged. "I don't think he took the poetry rules too seriously."

"Maybe he should have. Sounds to me like he lied to get the judging job and then he cheated."

"I don't know what to tell you."

Gertrude leaned back on the futon. "All right. Did he say anything else?"

"He was mad that it hadn't worked. Not only did Abby not fall all over him with gratitude, but she made him swear up and down not to tell anyone that he knew her."

"My," Gertrude said, "what a tangled web we weave."

21

"Now what?" Andrea asked as they crossed the parking lot toward her car.

"Now we go talk to Rose Waters's parents."

"Who is Rose Waters?" Andrea slid into the hot car.

"Another dead poet."

"And we're going to go bother her parents?"

"Not *bother* them, Andrea. *Help* them."

"How do you know where they live?"

"The newspaper gave the father's name. I looked him up on the Internet and found an address."

"Wow, so anybody can find anybody these days, right?"

"Almost," Gertrude said, musing about her mysterious Dave as she typed the address into her phone.

"You are on the fastest route," the phone chirped.

Minutes later, Andrea pulled into the sprawling driveway of a large suburban home. "This is a nice place."

"Yep," Gertrude agreed. "Pretty fancy place for Sexy Rose. They've even got a pool."

Andrea looked at her, alarmed. "You're not going to ask if you can go for a swim, are you?"

"Of course not. That's bonkers." Gertrude climbed out of the car, grabbed her walker from the back, and headed toward the front door. "Look! They've even got a fancy knocker thing." She picked it up and let it fall.

"Or you could just ring the doorbell."

"Oh," Gertrude said. "I didn't see that."

A middle-aged woman opened the door. Her hair was disheveled, and she had bags under her eyes. "Can I help you?"

"Are you Mrs. Waterford?" Gertrude asked.

"Yes. And you are?"

"My name is Gertrude. I am investigating your daughter's death—"

"What? Why?"

"Because I don't think it was an accident. May we come in?"

Mrs. Waterford hesitated. Then she held the door open. "Right this way. And please, call me Janet."

Gertrude stepped inside and immediately headed for the couch. Once she had settled in, she asked, "Were you home the night Rose died?"

Janet nodded. "I'm sorry. I don't understand. Who are you?"

"I'm Gertrude. I'm a gumshoe. This is my assistant, Andrea." Andrea stood awkwardly at the room's entrance.

Janet waited for Gertrude to say more. When she didn't, Janet said, "But why are you here? Roseanne's death was an accident. There's nothing to investigate. And what's your connection? Did someone call you?"

"Not exactly. I'm not so sure it was an accident. You see, there's been a string of suspicious deaths in your daughter's poetry club, and I think—"

"The police didn't say anything about that."

"Did the police come to your home?"

"Sure, though it was too late to do anything. We found Rose in the morning ..." Her voice broke and she looked down at her lap. Then she looked up, tears spilling from her eyes.

"Gertrude," Andrea said, "maybe we should go. We're upsetting a grieving mother here."

Janet swiped at her eyes. "No, no, it's OK." She swallowed hard. "It's good for me to talk about it, even if I don't understand why you want to know. You seem harmless enough." She smiled, but it looked forced. "My husband found her in the morning, in the pool. She was already cold. It was obvious she'd been dead for a while. We didn't know what we were supposed to do, so we called 911. Well, my husband, Roseanne's stepfather, did. And the police came. They asked a few questions, but they didn't say *anything* to indicate that her death was suspicious." She swallowed again. "What makes *you* think it was?"

"I don't know that it was, Janet. I just think it's strange that three poets have died within two weeks of each other. Did Rose live here?"

Janet nodded. Andrea took a box of tissues from the top of a piano and offered them to Janet. She took one and blew her nose into it. "She had recently moved back. She was having some money trouble."

"What did she do for work?"

"She tended bar." She gave a little shudder. "I hated it, but she said the tips were worth it. Anyway, she had a falling out with her roommate, so she moved back in here. Said she wanted to save up some money so she could get her own place without a roommate. Portland is so expensive. She wouldn't admit it, but I think she liked living here. She ate my food, watched my satellite stations, swam in my pool ..." The tears came in force then.

"What was her roommate's name?"

"Kyle. I don't know her last name. Just Kyle."

"So, did you see Rose the night she died?"

Janet nodded. "She had dinner with us. Then she went out."

"Where?"

Janet looked at her and Gertrude thought she'd never seen anyone look so miserable. "I don't know."

"Do you know when she came back?"

Janet shook her head and wiped at her eyes.

"Did she often swim alone in the middle of the night?"

Janet shook her head again. "She sure didn't. At least, not that I know of." She took a long, shaky breath. "As far as I know, she never once went swimming after dark. Guess that alone makes the situation a little suspicious, doesn't it?" She looked down at her lap.

"Maybe. Is there any reason to think that she was swimming alone?"

Janet's head snapped up. "You think she wasn't alone?"

"I don't know. But I think there's a good chance she was not."

22

Northbound on I-95, Gertrude asked, "Could I drive for a while?"

Andrea looked alarmed. "I thought you didn't have a license?"

"I don't. Yet. But I have a permit. And my test is coming up. And I should practice."

"I don't know, Gertrude."

"Just think. If I pass the test, you won't have to drive me around in the CAP bus anymore."

Andrea pulled off the next exit.

Gertrude slid into the driver's seat as if she'd done it a million times before. Remembering the eggshell, she put her right foot on the brake pedal and then put the car in drive. Smiling, she let the car roll to the park-n-ride exit. She came to a complete stop, looked both ways, and then pulled out into traffic, maybe a little too quickly. Inertia slammed their heads back into their headrests.

"Easy!" Andrea cried.

"It's all right! I'm a professional!"

Gertrude navigated the onramp and, after a few shaky swerves, settled into the right lane of the highway. She let out a breath she hadn't realized she'd been holding. "See? Not so bad."

"You're going thirty-five," Andrea muttered.

Gertrude looked down at the dash. "So I am. Let's see if we can get this old girl up to an even forty."

Andrea rolled her eyes.

"Hey, can you run a jitterbug?"

"You mean a phone?"

"Yes. A *smart*phone. Can you run a smartphone?"

"Probably. I have one, you know. You're not the only one in the world with a smartphone."

"Excellent. Would you open up that nifty YouTube app and look for Ashes LaFlamme?"

Andrea reached into her purse. "Sure. Why?"

"Because we're going to listen to some poems."

"I don't want to listen to poetry right now, Gertrude."

"We're not listening for the poetry. We're listening for clues."

Andrea was quiet as she navigated YouTube. Then, "Found her!"

"Excellent. Pick a poem. Any poem."

"Holy smokes, she's got a lot of 'em."

"Yep. I guess she's something of a pooh-bah."

"What?"

"Never mind. Just press play."

Within seconds, Ashes's familiar voice filled the car. As Gertrude drove north at exactly forty miles per hour, the two women listened carefully to a poem about unrequited love. When it was over, Andrea said, "That was awful. I didn't understand half of it, and the other half made me feel sick to my stomach."

"Yep. That one wasn't much help. Next."

Andrea pressed play. Ashes started to tell them about her abusive mother.

"I don't think this one is going to be much help. Next."

"That poor child," Andrea said.

"Don't get too shook up. It's just a poem. Doesn't mean it's true."

Ashes began to tell them about her favorite Mexican restaurant. This one made the women laugh. Who knew so many things could rhyme with guacamole?

"That one I understood, at least," Andrea said. "But I still don't understand why we're doing this at all. What clues do you expect to find hidden in YouTube poems?"

"Not sure we'll find any. But I'm very suspicious of Ashes, even though I also really like her. Part of me thinks she's the bad guy. Part of me wants to rule her out. Next poem, please."

The next poem was about competitive swimming.

"Well isn't that interesting?" Andrea said.

"Indeed. I didn't know she was a swimmer. But you know what's even more interesting? Listen to how angry she sounds.

How competitive. She sounds a little, I don't know, like she might come *unhinged*."

They listened to the swimming poem once more and then moved on to a poem about how hard it is to be a chemistry major and a poet, how Ashes felt she was living a double life, and none of the people in either life understood who she really was.

"Oh Mylanta!"

"What?" Andrea scrambled to press pause.

Gertrude looked at her wide-eyed. "She's a *chemistry major*?"

"Would you please look at the road!"

Gertrude looked ahead and saw that she was swerving onto the shoulder. She panicked and yanked the car to the left, overcorrecting directly into the path of the pickup currently trying to pass her. She jerked the wheel right and eventually settled into her own lane, her heart racing.

"Maybe it's good we're going thirty miles below the speed limit. Now, why do we care that she's a chemistry major?"

"Because maybe alcohol wasn't as big of a player as everyone thinks it was. John's blood alcohol level wasn't really that high. He *was* drinking, though, as were Abby and Rose. But maybe they weren't *just drunk*. Maybe they were just drunk enough so that they didn't notice taking something else, something stronger."

"You mean like a narcotic?"

"I mean like a poison."

"But doesn't poison show up in an autopsy?"

"It might. But I doubt they've done an autopsy with any of these people. They think they already know how they all died, right? So why an autopsy? The cops haven't suspected foul play." Gertrude tapped the wheel, thinking. "But she just said that she was a dean's list chemistry major. If that's true, I'm betting she would know of a poison that wouldn't show up on an autopsy."

"I think all poisons show up in an autopsy."

"Not if the autopsy's never performed."

23

Gertrude waited until the next morning to tell Calvin. It pained her to delay, but she was so tired by the time she got home from Portland, she could hardly keep her eyes open.

By morning, though, she was bright-eyed and bushy-tailed. After a quick shower and an even quicker breakfast, she headed out into the sunlight to visit Calvin.

He opened the door after only one knock. "Morning, Gert," he said, stepping back to allow her entrance.

"Your car's still gone."

"Yep. Takes a while to repair that much damage."

"Well is it going to be ready for Friday?"

"Why, what happens on Friday?"

"My road test."

"Your road test already?"

"Yep. Sent in for the date as soon as I got my permit."

"Well, yes, the car should be done by Friday, and no, you cannot use it in your road test."

"All right, well, we'll have to argue about that later. Right now, we've got bigger fish to broil."

Calvin chuckled. "OK, have a seat."

Gertrude sat on the couch.

"Wow," Calvin said.

"What?"

"I think that's the first time I've ever offered you a seat *before* you sat down. Want some coffee?"

"Sure, wise guy. Extra cream, extra sugar please."

"I don't have any cream. Skim milk OK?"

Gertrude curled her lip. "I suppose so."

"You look a little like Elvis when you do that."

"Really?"

"No, not really. So, what's the news?"

Gertrude filled him in: the Portland interviews; her coaching appointment with Ashes; and her suspicions about Little Miss Chemistry Major.

"She sure doesn't look like a chemistry major."

"Not when she's being a poet, no. But maybe she puts on her chemistry outfit when she's being a chemist. You know, she's like a carnelian."

"You mean a chameleon?" He handed her a steaming cup of coffee.

"Whatever. The lizard that changes colors. I'm not a lizard expert."

"You don't collect lizards?"

Gertrude's eyes grew wide with horror. "Of course not! That's gross, Calvin!"

Calvin shook his head, smiling. "All right then. So what's your plan?"

Gertrude took a sip of the coffee. "Well, I suppose I'm just going to have to get her to confess."

Calvin looked as if he was waiting for her to continue. When she didn't, he said, "And how do you plan to do that?'

"Still workin' on that part."

"I see."

"Well, we don't have a smoking gun this time. We don't even have any real clues. All we've got is a bunch of suspicious behavior. So I'm just going to try to get her talking and then see where it goes."

"I don't know, Gertrude. I think she might be more clever than our usual perpetrator. I'm not sure you're going to be able to trick her into confessing."

"I don't know as I was planning on *tricking* her. More like ..." Gertrude searched for the right word. "... *badgering* her into confessing."

Calvin chortled. "Yes, I can see that. All right then. So you've got a road test on Friday, and back to Portland on Monday? What are you going to do in the meantime?"

Gertrude groaned. "I suppose I have to write some more poems."

"You know, you don't *have* to compete. We could just go watch, now that you've established yourself as a poet—sort of. Or maybe you could just use the poems you've already used? I've heard lots of repeat poems and I've only been to two slams."

"Maybe," Gertrude said slowly. "And though those poems were fairly spectacular, I still think I can do better, and well, I'd rather go for the gold, as they say. I wouldn't mind qualifying. I've never been to Texas."

"Let's not get ahead of ourselves, Gertrude. Besides, what would your cats do with you in Texas?"

"They'd have to come along, of course."

24

Gertrude woke on Friday morning with a nagging feeling in her belly. She had forgotten something. Something important. Maybe even crucial. She went over and over her current case in her head, trying to figure out what was causing that blank spot in her brain.

It wasn't until she was on her way to Calvin's, and happened to glance at his repaired Cadillac, that it dawned on her. She had never exactly gotten Calvin to agree to letting her use the car for her road test. *Oh poo*, she thought. *I sure hope he's in a generous mood today.* She pounded on his door.

He opened it, which is always a good sign, but the look on his face told her that he knew exactly what she was going to ask.

"Please?"

He shook his head. "Gertrude, I just can't. That's an expensive car! And well, you don't *know how to drive!* Are you sure you're even ready for a road test? Maybe you could get it postponed."

She pushed past him into his trailer. "I'm ready, Calvin! I drove Andrea's car all the way home from Portland!"

An eyebrow went up, and she saw a chink in his armor. "You did?"

"I did. I can drive, Calvin, and they're not even going to let me do anything hard in the test. I won't even go on the interstate. You can drive me there and back. I will only be in the driver's seat for about ten minutes, and the tester person will be right there the whole time. What could possibly go wrong?"

He was quiet. He was thinking it over. She tried not to smile.

"When you drove Andrea's car, how did that go?"

"It went fine."

"Did you hit anything?"

Gertrude folded her arms across her chest. "Of course not."

"All right then. But! This doesn't mean you can drive my car ever again. This might well be a one-time thing. I'm going against my better judgment here because I realize you don't have a lot of options."

"Thank you kindly, Calvin. Now, if you're ready, we should get going."

"Right now?"

"Right now."

"Geesh, you didn't give yourself any wiggle room, did you?"

"What?"

"I mean, what if I hadn't caved?"

Gertrude shrugged. "I would've just called my other assistant."

Calvin guffawed. "Sure. Let me get my feet dressed."

Despite Calvin's propensity for punctuality, he pulled into the BMV parking lot at 10:02 for Gertrude's ten o'clock appointment. She considered complaining but didn't want to take any more time.

She headed toward the glass door, not waiting for Calvin to catch up, but he did anyway, and opened the door for her.

"Ah," Gertrude said blissfully.

"What?"

"Air conditioning." She approached the help desk and identified herself.

"You're late," a sour-faced woman announced. Her nametag read Sally.

"Sorry, I had a sick cat," Gertrude lied.

Sally nodded, her lips pressed together into a thin, pale line, and asked Gertrude for her identification and permit, which Gertrude provided.

"Please step over here," Sally said, motioning to a line taped to the floor.

Gertrude placed her toes on the line.

"Can you read the third line down on the eye chart?"

"Of course I can."

Sally waited. Then, "Would you, please?"

"Oh. Sure." Gertrude read the line.

Sally looked impressed. "Great job. You see well."

"Yep. Like a hawk in heat."

Sally actually laughed. "You can go have a seat right over there." She nodded toward a waiting area, where Calvin had already settled. "Someone will be right with you."

Gertrude sat.

"Why do these chairs have to be bolted to the floor?" Calvin said. "Makes me feel like I'm in prison."

"You ever been to prison, Calvin?"

"Of course not. Don't be ridiculous. But really, are they afraid I'm going to steal a chair from the BMV?"

"Probably more afraid someone will fail their test and throw a chair at the meanieface behind the counter."

Calvin snickered. "It looked like you were getting along with her all right."

"No, not Sally. I wouldn't throw a chair at her. I just meant your average BMV meanieface."

"Ah, I see."

A man approached them. "Gertrude?"

She nodded and stood.

He looked at her walker and then looked at her. "All right then. Let's go to your vehicle."

Gertrude looked at Calvin. "You going to wait here?"

"Yes. But I'm also going outside to watch."

Gertrude started toward the door. "You going to chase us around Skowhegan?" she said without turning around.

No one responded to her, and when they got outside, Calvin sat at a smoking area picnic table and put his head in his hands. He looked as if he might be praying.

The tester, who identified himself as Bob, followed Gertrude to the car, and waited patiently for her to stow her walker in the backseat. When she got into the front, he followed suit.

His unwavering attention unnerved Gertrude. *Why is he staring at me?* She started the car and looked at him. He continued to stare. *What a weirdo.* He jotted something down on his clipboard. She put the car in reverse and, without looking in her mirrors or over her shoulder, put her foot on the gas. She remembered Calvin's eggshell rule, so they only gently lurched forward as she backed up; still, this lurching startled Gertrude, so she slammed her foot onto the brake pedal, effectively squashing any imaginary egg and slamming both their heads into the headrest. Bob's eyebrows shot up near his hairline as he made another note. Gertrude, for the first time, felt a niggling.

"What do you keep writing down?"

"Just concentrate on your driving."

"Fine." She eased the car out of the parking lot and then, though there was no car coming from either direction, she floored it and yanked the car onto the road, forcing their heads back to their headrests.

For a quarter of a mile, Gertrude drove like a seasoned driver. She crossed a short bridge and came to a complete stop at the stop sign at the end of it.

A tractor trailer truck was signaling to turn left onto the bridge, and he had the right of way, but instead of turning, he stopped in the middle of the road and furiously motioned for Gertrude to turn in front of him.

She didn't know what to do.

"You've stopped too far forward, so he can't make the turn. Just go ahead and go," Bob said.

"But I'm stopped at the stop sign!"

"Just go."

She went. Without signaling. Or checking to see if someone was coming from the left. Someone was. A three-quarter-ton pickup. And she never saw it.

She heard it first, and thought it was the tractor trailer driver blowing his horn. She had just a second to think, *I know, I know, I'm going!*

Then she felt the impact, as the truck smashed into the back half of Calvin's car and sent Gertrude and Bob into a counterclockwise spin.

Gertrude opened her mouth to scream, but then the airbag deployed, and everything went dark.

25

Gertrude woke in the ambulance. She looked around for Calvin, but her only company was a single paramedic.

"How are you feeling?" he asked.

"Just dandy. I didn't kill Bob, did I?"

"No one died in the accident. Who is Bob?"

"The man who was in the car with me. He was giving me a driver's test. I think I might not have passed."

"Bob will be OK. He's on his way to the hospital in a separate ambulance."

"Did he say anything about me passing?"

Gertrude wasn't sure, but it looked as though the paramedic might have suppressed a smirk. "He didn't. Sorry."

Gertrude's back hurt and it felt as if small, invisible people were stabbing knives into her head, so she decided to close her eyes and stop talking. She kept her eyes closed as expert arms extracted her from the ambulance and then pushed her through the hospital's automatic doors. She answered a nurse's questions with staccato no's and yep's, and then she gave the same responses to a doctor who asked the same questions. She downplayed her soreness because all she really wanted was to go home and allow herself to be buried in cats.

Finally, a nurse gave her the green light. Awash with relief, she sat up and looked around for her walker. It was nowhere to be seen. She called after the nurse who had just left and learned that her walker must not have been recovered from the accident yet.

"Hang tight. I'll go find you another walker."

"I don't want another walker!" Gertrude screeched. "I want *my* walker!"

"Sure, sure," the nurse said soothingly. "You can get it back when you get your car back. You'll have to just call the police and find out where the car was towed."

Gertrude didn't hear the second half of her sentence, as she realized she would have to go through Calvin to get her walker, and she thought maybe Calvin wasn't very happy with her right now. "All right, all right. By the way, you haven't seen my friend Calvin here, have you?"

"There was an older gentleman here asking about you, but he left a while ago."

"He left?"

"Yes, he said he just wanted to make sure you were going to be all right." The nurse smiled and left Gertrude sitting on the side of her bed, wondering how she was ever going to get home. She certainly couldn't call Calvin. He had already left her. The clock told her it was after seven, which meant the CAP bus was done for the day. She thought about calling Andrea but didn't know her number. This left her church, but she didn't know that number either.

She saw a woman in scrubs walk by her open doorway. "Nurse!" she hollered.

The woman backpedaled and looked at her through the open doorway. "Yes?"

"Is there a phonebook around here?"

"We have one at the nurse's station. Can I look up a number for you?"

"Open Door Church, please."

Maggie, the church secretary and cosmetologist, pulled up alongside the hospital twenty minutes later, and found Gertrude waiting in a wheelchair.

Gertrude stood up as Maggie got out of her minivan.

"Where's your purse?" Maggie asked, and Gertrude knew she was referring to the walker pouch.

"I suppose it's still in Calvin's car." Gertrude hobbled to the minivan, hating every step. *This walker just feels so ... so ... wrong.*

"You OK?" Maggie's round eyes were full of concern.

"Fit as a fiddle." Gertrude slid into the passenger seat. She tried to shut the car door, but Maggie stopped her.

"I meant emotionally."

Gertrude curled her upper lip. "I'm fine."

"OK, Gertrude."

Gertrude slammed the door and let Maggie put the loaner walker into the back.

When they got to Gertrude's trailer, Maggie offered to help her inside, but Gertrude balked. *I can take care of myself, thank you very much.* Gertrude painfully climbed the few steps to her door and then went inside. She fed her cats and then lay down to rest.

It took the entire weekend for Gertrude's body to stop aching from the crash, so she spent it inside. Besides, she didn't want to go anywhere without her walker, and she wasn't sure how to go about getting it back.

26

By Monday morning, Gertrude had recovered, at least physically, from her road test. And she had decided she would still pursue the case, even if she didn't have her walker—or Calvin. (She hadn't seen hide nor hair of him since her road test.) She just needed to find a way to get to Portland. She knew the CAP bus wouldn't take her all the way to Portland, for any reason, but she called it anyway, praying that Andrea was driving.

She wasn't. It was Norm. Normally, this would please her. But right now, she needed Andrea.

"Hi, Norm."

"Hey, Gertrude." He paused. "Aren't you going to get in?"

"No, thanks. Hey, I need to talk to Andrea. Do you have her number?"

"You called me out here to ask me for Andrea's phone number?"

"Yes."

"I can't say I'm too thrilled with that, Gertrude."

Gertrude felt nothing even closely resembling remorse. "I really need to talk to her, Norm."

"Well, I don't have her number. And even if I did, I wouldn't give it to you."

Gertrude gasped. "How rude!"

Norman rolled his eyes.

Gertrude climbed into the van. "Then take me to her house."

"No!"

"No?"

"No! I'm not taking you to her house. She's a volunteer. I'm not going to help you harass her. Besides, I don't even know where she lives."

"I do."

"Gertrude, *no.*"

Gertrude did some quick thinking. "Fine. Can you please take me to the Episcopal church?"

Norman looked at her in the rearview mirror. "You're not Episcopalian."

"Just converted. Now let's go."

Norman sighed and put his hand on the shifter. "I'm guessing Andrea lives near the Episcopal church?"

"The less you know, the better, Norm."

Norman dropped her off in the empty church parking lot. She thanked him and then stood still, waiting for him to drive away. She waved as he did, and then she headed into the woods. She cut across a small pine grove and came out in Andrea's back yard, where Andrea was back-to, hanging laundry on a clothesline.

Gertrude tapped her on the back.

Andrea let out a little screech and jumped about three inches off the ground. Then she looked at Gertrude and swore.

"Potty mouth!" Gertrude said, aghast.

"Gertrude, you scared the devil out of me!"

"I need you to drive me to Portland."

"What?"

"Tonight is the poetry slam. And I'm supposed to go for an early coaching session with Ashes—"

"Ashes? Who's Ashes again?"

"She's the killer. So I'll need you to pick me up at three. All right?"

Andrea looked incredulous, but she nodded. "A poetry slam? So we're going to the thing that gets people killed?"

"Not all people. Just poets. You'll be fine. So, see you at three?"

Andrea nodded again and reached down for a wet bath towel as Gertrude headed back toward the pine grove.

***

Andrea arrived at Gertrude's trailer an hour early.

"Well aren't you just a Johnny-on-the-spot," Gertrude said after opening the door.

"I thought maybe we should discuss the case before we go."

"The case?"

"Yes. I've read a lot of murder mysteries in my day. I might be able to be of some help."

"I don't need any help. I already know who the murderer is."

"You said that. But can you tell me about what evidence you have? What's her—"

A knock on the door interrupted.

Gertrude gave Andrea an accusing look. "Did you invite someone else?"

Andrea shook her head. "I have manners, you know."

Gertrude headed toward the door, and after opening it, nearly fell backward in surprise.

There Calvin stood, leaning on her walker. "Don't you want this?"

"Well, yes, of course—"

"May I come in?"

Gertrude stepped out of the way.

Calvin stepped inside and stared at Andrea for several seconds. Then he looked at Gertrude. "I see you've replaced me?"

"What?"

"Well, I thought I was your partner. But apparently I was just your driver. So now that you've totaled my car, you just forget all about me?"

Gertrude didn't know whether to laugh at him or hug him. "I didn't forget about you, Calvin. I thought you were mad at me."

"I am mad at you."

"Can I have my walker?"

Calvin gave it to her, and Gertrude leaned on it gratefully. It felt like chocolate pudding after a fast.

"Do you two need a minute?" Andrea asked.

"No," they said in unison. Then they both stood there silently, looking at each other.

"Well?" Calvin asked.

"Well what?"

"Is she going to drive you to Portland?"

Gertrude wasn't sure how to respond. So she decided to go with the truth. "Yes."

As she'd expected, Calvin looked hurt at this admission. "And what about me?"

"Do you want to come too?" Gertrude asked.

"Aren't I your partner?"

Gertrude preferred the term "assistant," but figured this was no time to split hairs.

"Absolutely. So you should come too."

"All right. I will." Calvin looked at Andrea. "Can I ride up front?"

27

On the way south, Calvin and Gertrude filled Andrea in on everything they knew about the case: They weren't sure there'd even been a murder, but they *thought* there'd been several. They also figured Ashes had tried to cheat in a slam and had gotten caught. So she'd killed her co-conspirator judge and the poet who'd caught them. And for some reason, she'd also killed Rose Waters, maybe just because she posed a competitive threat. They weren't sure how she was killing people, but they thought she was using some sort of poison that wouldn't necessarily show up in an autopsy.

"You know this all sounds a little far-fetched, right?" Andrea asked at one point.

"Truth is stranger than fiction" was Calvin's reply.

"So what's the plan?" Andrea asked.

Gertrude, well beyond annoyed at having to sit in the backseat with her walker, said, "Not sure yet. Just going to get her talking."

"You don't have to holler, Gertrude. You're in the backseat, not the car behind us."

"Wouldn't know it the way you two are leaving me out."

"So, you're just going to try to get her to admit it?" Andrea asked doubtfully.

"You'd be surprised," Calvin said. "Gertrude can be pretty persuasive when she tries."

They used Gertrude's GPS to find the Eastern Prom, and they found Ashes waiting at the gazebo.

As they slowly approached, Ashes called out, "You brought friends?"

"These are my fans," Gertrude said, and she thought she heard Calvin groan.

"I didn't realize I was going to be coaching in front of an audience." Ashes didn't sound pleased.

"They won't listen. They don't really care about poetry," Gertrude said.

"I thought you just said they were your fans?"

"Well, they like *my* poetry, but not poetry in general."

"Hazel," Calvin muttered, "you're not making any sense."

"Shh," Gertrude hissed. "Let me handle this." She climbed the gazebo steps and then looked at Ashes triumphantly. "All right. What do you want to do first?"

"First, let's try a breathing exercise."

"What? Why?"

"Because breathing is very important on stage, and it will help you deliver with more poise and volume."

"All right. Whatever. Teach me to breathe."

Ashes directed Gertrude to sit cross-legged on the floor. "Criss-cross applesauce," she said.

Gertrude managed to sit, but her legs wouldn't fold the way Ashes's legs did. Gertrude crossed her ankles and looked at Ashes. "This will have to do."

Calvin and Andrea sat on a bench and silently watched Ashes and Gertrude breathe together. After several minutes of slow inhales and thorough exhales, Ashes offered Gertrude some iced rosemary tea.

Gertrude scrunched up her nose. "No, thanks."

"No, have some. It will balance your solar plexus chakra—"

"My what?"

Ashes held the glass jar out toward Gertrude. "It will give you confidence and calm any anxiety—"

"I have plenty of confidence and I don't have any anxiety."

"Just try it." She pushed the jar toward Gertrude.

"Did Abby ever drink any of your poetry tea?"

"What?"

"I'm just wondering if my cousin ever drank any of this ... this ..." She resisted the urge to say "potion." "... this *concoction* of yours."

"I don't know. Maybe?"

"What about Rose?"

Ashes looked as if she'd been slapped. But she didn't respond.

"Did you ever give Rose anything to drink?"

Ashes shook her head. "Why don't we get started?" she said, getting up.

Gertrude wasn't positive, but she thought she saw tears in Ashes's eyes. But trying to confirm this led to an awkward moment of a ready Ashes towering over a still seated unready Gertrude. "Calvin, help me up."

Calvin got up, walked around so he stood in front of her, and then took her hand in his and pulled.

"Easy!" she cried. "I'm not a sack of taters!" She was standing by the time she finished her remark and leaned gratefully on her walker. "Thank you, Calvin." She turned her attention to Ashes. "What's next, coach?"

"Why don't we run through one of your poems. Perform it as if you were competing, and I'll give you some constructive feedback."

"All right. How well did you know Rose Waters?"

Ashes didn't respond. She gave Gertrude a long look, and then she looked at the ceiling as a single tear escaped down her cheek. "You know what? I'm sorry, Hazel, I just can't do this today. I'm not feeling so well. I'll see you at the reading." Before Gertrude could respond, Ashes had scooped up her bag and her jar of rosemary tea and ran off across the park.

As the three of them watched her go, Calvin said, "Well, that went well."

"Now what?" Andrea asked.

159

"Not sure. We've still got an hour and a half until the reading starts," Gertrude said. Then she had a thought. "Andrea! Will you take us to Goodwill?"

28

One polka-dot skort, one tennis racket, and two salt and pepper shaker sets later, Gertrude, Calvin, and Andrea were back in the Subaru.

"What are you going to do with a tennis racket, Gertrude?" Andrea asked.

"Put it with my other tennis rackets."

Calvin groaned, but he managed to sound amused while he did so.

"What? You never know when there's going to be a crisis that requires a tennis racket. All right, Andrea. It's the moment we've all been waiting for. Let's go to that poetry slam!"

Andrea pulled out of the Goodwill parking lot and headed back toward the Old Port. As they started bouncing along the cobblestone streets, Gertrude tried to help Andrea find a parking spot.

"How about you *don't* help with the driving, Gertrude?" Calvin snipped.

Gertrude crossed her arms and leaned back in the seat to sulk as Andrea expertly tucked her car into a tiny parallel parking spot. Then they all climbed out of the car and headed up the hill toward Alfonso's.

They were the first ones to enter the basement room. Andrea let out a fearful gasp. Jade looked them up and down and then gave them a huge smile along with her "Welcome!" She looked at Gertrude. "Will you be slamming tonight, Hazel?"

"With bells on," Gertrude said as she stooped to the sign-up sheet. Then she headed toward the back of the room, without offering anyone any money, leaving Calvin to pay her admission. She didn't know who paid for Andrea and she didn't care. She wanted to talk to the bartender. She leaned on the empty bar. "Hiya, barkeep."

He didn't acknowledge her presence.

"Can you tell me what kind of a relationship Ashes LaFlamme and Rose Waters had?"

Without looking at her, he said, "Lady, I don't pay any attention to these people's lives. Can I get you a drink?"

Calvin appeared beside her. "I'll take a glass of merlot, please."

The bartender nodded.

Calvin sat at the bar and drank wine, chatting with Andrea, while Gertrude watched the room fill up. She was practically praying for suspicious behavior, but she didn't see any. At least, not anything more suspicious than weeks prior. She watched

Bae Drew hug his way across the room and when he got to her, he didn't alter his pattern.

"Can I give you a big hug, Hazel?" She didn't respond and soon couldn't, as her face was smashed into his shoulder. He held her for at least ten seconds before letting her go. "It's so good to see you again! Will you be reading tonight?"

"Does a bear poop in the woods?"

Bae laughed as if that was the funniest thing he'd ever heard, and then sauntered off to find someone else to hug. Gertrude continued to people watch, and soon noticed Ashes arriving. She let out a deep breath she didn't realize she'd been holding. "Calvin," she said, tugging on his sleeve. "Ashes is here. Let's go sit near her."

"You go ahead. I'm staying close to the wine."

Gertrude hesitated.

"I'll come with you!" Andrea chirped.

"All right." Gertrude headed into the center of the growing crowd and plopped down in a chair beside Ashes, who shifted, almost imperceptibly, away from her. "Ashes, I just wanted to say I'm sorry about before. I didn't mean to upset you."

"I don't really want to talk about it, Hazel."

"All right. You slamming tonight?"

"Don't need to. I'm already qualified."

"Oh. That's right. So who are you rooting for?"

"Don't care. I'll beat whoever wins in the finals." Ashes got up and moved to a row of tall pub tables along the wall and sat down at one, across from Alec.

"Well, she's unpleasant," Andrea muttered.

"Most murderers are," Gertrude said. Andrea sat beside her, and the two women stayed put as the chairs filled up around them. Gertrude kept one eye on Ashes and one on everyone else.

Before long, Beth called the evening to order. "Welcome to Poetland, poets! We're glad you're here. We're going to have an open mic, and then we're going to have our last chance slam! That means tonight is your very last chance to qualify for the individual semifinals! We still have one slot left, so if you haven't signed up yet ..."

As the crowd hooted and hollered, Gertrude raised one suggestive eyebrow at Calvin. The thought of Calvin on stage made her giddy.

He ignored her.

"So, let's get started with our open mic!" Beth instructed people to keep their performances short and their phones off, punctuating her reminders with multiple profanities.

"Oh dear," Andrea muttered.

"You ain't seen nothin' yet," Gertrude said.

The open mic lasted nearly two hours. Gertrude listened closely to each poem, trying to find a clue, but there were no poems about guilt, no poems about murder, and no mention of any dead poets. She was profoundly disappointed.

When it was time for the slam, Gertrude headed toward the corner to draw her number. Her heart wasn't really in it this time, but she figured competing would be more exciting than

164

not competing. She drew the three. Blaine was back, appeared to be sober, drew the four, and then ate the number. Disgusted, Gertrude stopped paying attention to the draw.

Returning to her seat, she found Andrea looking around in wonder.

"This is so neat!" Andrea said. "Are you going to keep coming to these events even after you solve the murder?"

"Not sure. Depends on how busy my next case keeps me."

Beth called the calibration poet to the stage. She read a poem about bread pudding. This made Gertrude's stomach growl loudly enough that she was afraid the row in front of them would turn to glare. They didn't.

The first competing poet, Thor, performed a poem about fixing up his father's car, and received abysmal scores.

"Oh, that poor man," Andrea said. "That must be so devastating."

"I think he's used to it," Gertrude said.

Zest was next. She recited a poem about the paintings in cheap motels. It was actually pretty funny, and everyone laughed, but the judges remained unimpressed.

"Are the judges always this mean?" Andrea whispered.

"No, they love me."

Beth called Gertrude up to the stage. She got up and headed toward the mic, but out of the corner of her eye, she thought she saw Ashes slip something into Alec's drink. Then she saw him pick up his glass. Without thinking about what she was doing, she veered off course and ran across the room, stepping on feet, purses, books, and anything else that got in her way, reached Alec just as his lips were about to touch the glass, and swatted the glass out of his hand. The glass flew to her left and shattered onto the floor.

29

Alec looked at Gertrude, his eyes like Frisbees. Then he swore.

"Watch your mouth, young'un. I just saved your life."

"Saved it from what?" Alec hollered, standing up. Even though Gertrude was the shortest person in the room, Alec was still only a few inches taller than her, so they stood nearly eye-to-eye, his spiked mohawk towering over them.

The room was so silent, one could almost hear the chopsticks clicking upstairs.

"From her!" Gertrude cried and pointed at Ashes.

Ashes rolled her eyes and swore at Gertrude. Then she looked at Beth, who was still standing in front of the microphone. "Are you going to do something? This lunatic just assaulted Alec!"

Gertrude felt a hand on her right elbow and turned to see it belonged to the bouncer. She ripped it out of his hands so hard her shoulder hurt. "Don't touch me! Can't you see I'm fighting crime!" She looked at Alec. "I just saw Ashes put something in your drink! And seeings how she's already poisoned three other poets and tried to poison Blaine, I would think that would concern you!"

Alec was speechless. Ashes wasn't. "Why would I poison *Blaine*?" she asked, as if that was the only absurd thing Gertrude had suggested.

"Why would you poison anyone?" Gertrude screeched. "How should I know? Because you're a cutthroat psychopath chemist!"

Someone behind Gertrude started snapping their fingers, and though she found that strange, it also pleased her.

"Who did she poison?" Alec asked.

Ashes turned her glare on him. "I didn't poison anyone!"

"She killed Abby, John, and Rose, and she tried to kill Blaine!" Gertrude declared.

"She didn't kill anyone!" came a high-pitched tremor from across the room. "I did!"

Every head in the room turned toward the source of that sound and found Bae standing near the piano. "It was me!"

People were silent as they digested this, until Gertrude broke the stillness with a disgusted, "No you didn't!"

Bae looked stunned.

"Why would you kill those people?" Gertrude demanded.

"Because I love Ashes!"

Someone near the front moaned as if they'd just heard some particularly moving line of poetry, and someone else began to snap their fingers.

"You *love* Ashes?" Gertrude asked.

"I do. And I wanted her to win. So I killed them all."

"Why did you kill John?" Gertrude demanded.

Bae didn't answer.

"And how do you know how to poison people? Are you a chemistry major too?"

Bae looked at the floor.

Gertrude pointed at Bae with her right hand and said to the crowd, "He did not kill John." Then she pointed at Ashes with her left hand. "She did!" With both arms outstretched, Gertrude wobbled a little, and grabbed for her walker to steady herself. Then she looked at the crowd again. "On July 3, Ashes recruited John Crane to be a judge. She was trying to fix the slam. She offered him sexual favors in exchange for good scores—"

Dozens of onlookers gasped at this, but none as loudly as Ashes herself. "I would never!"

"Hm," Gertrude said, lowering her voice dramatically. "You just looked very convincing, Ashes. Much more convincing than when you said you didn't kill him! I wonder why that is." She put her hand to her chin and tried to feign a thinking-hard expression.

"Did you sleep with that guy?" Bae asked.

"No!" Ashes cried. She was looking around the room like a rabbit caught in a trap.

"So why did you kill Abby?" Alec asked.

"I didn't!"

"I *saw* you key their car, Ashes!" Alec said.

More gasps sounded around the room.

"She killed Abby because Abby found out about the cheating!" Gertrude said.

A few seconds of silence allowed the room to digest this revelation. Beth still stood at the microphone as if she'd forgotten her lines. Alec looked smug. Ashes looked enraged. Bae looked brokenhearted.

Finally, Ashes, her face lobster-red, said, "I did not kill anyone. None of this makes any sense. I came in third at nationals last year. I don't need to kill people to win slams."

"Actually," a voice came from the back of the room.

"Blaine, don't," Ashes pleaded.

"I wouldn't, Ashes, but this has gone far enough. I was going to take your secret to the grave, but you're killing people now?"

"I'm not—" she started.

"What secret?" Gertrude demanded.

Blaine looked at the floor. "Ashes fixed the judges at nationals."

This revelation brought the most powerful gasps thus far, and Beth finally said, "I think it's time to call the police." The bartender nodded and picked up the phone.

"We don't need to call the police," Ashes tried.

"Yes, we do. Because I'm admitting that I killed these people." Bae was crying now, giant tears rolling down his cheeks.

Blaine started across the room toward Bae, and the people parted to let him walk through. "Bae, stop. We know you couldn't hurt anyone. We also know you're in love with Ashes. But that doesn't mean you have to cover for her." He put one hairy, burly arm around Bae's shoulders. "And you really shouldn't fall on your sword for someone who won't at least try to stop you from doing so."

Every head in the room turned toward Ashes, as if waiting for her to rescue Bae from himself.

Ashes did not do so. Instead, she glared at Gertrude. "You are such a nut. You're just making a bunch of ridiculous accusations and hoping one of them sticks. Why would I poison Blaine? He is not a threat to me, or to anyone else for that matter. He's a terrible poet."

Several people booed this, but Ashes just raised her voice. "And I wouldn't kill Rose. I loved her. And besides, she was already qualified."

"You loved her?" Bae shrieked.

Ashes softly swore as a look of clarity washed over her face.

"What is it?" Gertrude asked. "What did you just figure out?"

"You," Ashes said softly, looking at Bae. "You killed her."

"Of course I did!" Bae spat. "I knew you were falling for her, I knew you were going to tell her your secrets, and I knew she couldn't be trusted to keep them! And even if she did, I couldn't let her steal you away from me!"

"I wasn't yours!"

"But you would've been!"

Blaine tried to convince Bae to stop talking.

"You killed Rose?" Gertrude asked Bae.

Bae crumpled into his chair, sobbing. He gave a small nod. "But I didn't kill Abby or John. Ashes did."

Jade stood up. "I think she did. And I think I can prove it."

"You cannot!" Ashes screamed.

The crowd stared at Jade. "Abby told me she was going to report Ashes. I tried to talk her out of it, but she was so stubborn. Abby told me that she was going to go out with Ashes the night she died. She was laughing, said she knew that Ashes was going to buy her a bunch of drinks and try to talk her out of it. She said it didn't matter what Ashes did, that she was still going to report her, but that she might as well have the free drinks."

"That doesn't prove anything," Ashes said through clenched teeth.

"Maybe not. But I think I can give a pretty convincing testimony. I am a poet, after all."

There was a pause, and then someone behind Gertrude started a slow, loud clap. She turned to find Ned nodding along with his beat. Then others joined in, and soon most of the room was applauding. Gertrude wasn't sure why they were clapping, but she thought she should respond, so she gave a quick curtsy.

30

"Gertrude?"

Gertrude started. She'd almost been asleep, leaning on her window in the backseat. She wiped a spot of drool from the corner of her mouth. "Yes, Calvin?"

"Can we please never go to another poetry reading again?"

Gertrude thought for a second. "I don't think we need to go unless someone starts killing poets again."

"Even if they do, I think we should stay out of it. I think I prefer my poetry in books. Where it rhymes. And makes sense. And is written by dead people. Who died from natural causes."

Gertrude leaned back against the window. "That's fine, Calvin."

"Is it wrong to hope that the next crime wave happens close to home?" Calvin said thoughtfully.

"Probably." Gertrude closed her eyes.

"I don't know," Andrea said. "I thought tonight was fun. It was certainly exciting. I mean, I'm not excited that I'm now driving home from Portland, but other than that, it was a fun night. Do you think they're going to be able to convict Ashes?"

"Dunno," Gertrude said. "Our job is to figure out whodunit. We'll let the cops worry about prosecution."

"Our job?" Calvin said mockingly. "Thanks for clarifying that. Until just now, I had no idea what *our job* was." He laughed.

"We still don't know who poisoned Blaine," Andrea said.

"About that," Calvin said, "he spoke to me before we left. Told me he'd taken some recreational drugs that night and asked me not to tell the cops. Asked me to just tell them that he'd had a lot to drink."

"So no one poisoned Blaine?"

"Guess not," Calvin said. "And no one was trying to poison Alec either."

"What do you mean?" Gertrude asked.

Andrea slowed down for the toll booth. "Do you have any money?" she asked Calvin.

He groaned and reached for his wallet. "I mean, I was staring right at Ashes before you made your big scene. She didn't put anything in Alec's drink. I don't know what you think you saw."

"Oh," Gertrude said. Then she lied, "I didn't think I saw anything. I was just trying to get her talking. I told you that was the plan."

"Uh-huh," Calvin said, sounding skeptical.

Andrea drove out of the toll booth, rolling up her window. "Do you guys think maybe I could help you with your next case?"

"Sure," Gertrude said. "The more the merrier. So long as you understand I'm in charge. I'm the gumshoe."

Calvin was silent.

"Calvin?"

"Yes, Gertrude?"

"I'm really sorry about your car."

"You should be."

"I didn't mean to crash it."

"I know you didn't."

"Do you have enough money to get it fixed?"

"I have insurance. But I don't think I'm going to get it fixed."

A small panic settled in Gertrude's belly. "No?"

"I think I'm just going to get a new vehicle, and I was actually wondering ..."

Gertrude waited for him to continue. "About?"

"Well, I'm not sure a Cadillac is the best vehicle for fighting crime. I was thinking maybe we should do some brainstorming because I'm not sure what *would* be the best vehicle. I mean, we should get something that blends into our surroundings, for stakeouts and such. But we'll want something fast in case we have to chase someone. But we'll also need four-wheel drive, for winter crime fighting, right?"

Gertrude leaned her head back, smiling from ear to ear. She'd never been so excited in her whole life.

The Gert Books

Made in the USA
Middletown, DE
27 July 2023